I0722211

STOLEN BY MONSTERS

FALLING FOR THE ENEMY (BOOK ONE)

LUNA PIERCE

STOLEN BY MONSTERS

Copyright © 2021 by Luna Pierce and Kate Myers

All rights reserved.

No part of this book may be reproduced in any form or by any electronic or mechanical means, including information storage and retrieval systems, without written permission from the author, except for the use of brief quotations in a book review.

This is a work of fiction. Names, characters, places, and incidents either are the product of the author's imagination or are used fictitiously. Any resemblance to actual persons, living or dead, events, or locales is entirely coincidental.

Book Cover Design by Night Witch
Proofing by Tiffany Hernandez and Cruel Ink Editing
First Edition 2021
ASIN B09RHYWWDC (ebook)
ISBN 978-1-957238-03-6 (Paperback)

To those of you who love a good ol' enemies to lovers romance. I gotchu.

I

WREN

Warm and thick blood trickles out of my nose and gurgles its way up my throat and into my mouth.

I lay there, face down, silent, and motionless on the cold, hard, dirty floor.

I don't dare open my eyes. According to the pain coursing through my body, I'm convinced that I've fractured multiple bones.

I'm not sure I could move if I wanted to.

I was once a feared assassin, and now I'm a broken mess scattered at the base of these stairs in an old, abandoned building on the outskirts of a run-down town.

I wait for death—slow and cruel in her sadistic manner. But she takes her time, taunting me from the sweet release only she could bring.

"Is she alive?" A male voice whispers.

"I...I don't think so," the other person responds.

His tone is smooth and angelic with something resembling concern weaved in.

One of the men approaches, so close I can smell the sweet scent of honey on his breath. Such a contrast to the dirt and decay of this end of the forgotten city.

But there's nothing sweet about him. I'm in enemy territory and this can only mean one thing—he's come to finish me off.

I did something I never do; I made a mistake...a slip up that cost me everything. And now, not only did I miss my target, but I'm going to meet the same fate that was intended for him.

If only death would stop playing games and hurry up and take me from this disgusting place and save me from whatever torture I'm about to endure.

Despite my best efforts to play dead, I choke on the red metallic mess coating my mouth.

One of the people gasps. Or maybe it was both. I can't be certain with the ringing in my ears and throbbing in my head.

Cool hands find their way under my frame, gently tilting me to the side.

I keep my eyes shut. There's no need to witness what will happen next.

I'm no stranger to gore but being on the receiving end of it is never any fun.

Unless it's consensual, then that's a different story entirely.

I stifle a curse that rolls off my tongue and wince at the new wave of pain coursing through me at the change in positions.

Why couldn't they just leave me there to die alone, semi-peacefully?

Haven't they already done enough damage?

I know better than to expect anything different out of their kind. Vile, demented creatures who do nothing but torment and taint our world with their bloodlust and desire to take what is not theirs. They kill without cause, wiping out entire villages and leaving no innocent spared. It's those like me who are tasked to eliminate them in an attempt to even the playing field and protect the balance. The demons and their bringers are the evil that must be purged from our world.

I have trained for this position my entire life. And I have worked tirelessly the last four years to wipe out every target I've been assigned. Up until today, I have had a complete success rate, killing more of them than I can count and saving many lives in the process.

I rose through the ranks swiftly, becoming the acclaimed *Furla Ain* only two years into my post.

Most feared assassin.

My name is respected, carries great terror, and is something I take immense pride in.

What a disgrace I am, my limp body being carried out of here by the enemy.

Everything hurts. Every inch this creature takes is another blip of sharp pain, dull pain, fierce pain.

I clench my jaw, desperately trying to disassociate myself from the agony and somehow, it only brings more.

How I'm still alive is a mystery in itself. I should be dead from the injuries alone, and yet, here I am, writhing through the torment.

Don't get me wrong, in any other situation I'd be grateful...but knowing I'm in bad company means the suffering has only just begun. Whatever they have in store for me will be much worse than the trauma I've already experienced.

"Wes, what are you doing?" The one guy asks the other.

His core tightens along with his grip on me. "I don't know."

"We...we aren't taking her, are we?"

"We can't leave her there."

"Since when?" The person shuffles closer.

"Let it go, Dash. We'll talk about it at home."

Home? He's taking me to where they live? This can't be good. I must do something, anything.

I wiggle under his grip, doing everything I can to garner the strength to move. Maybe if I free myself, I can drop to the ground and my injuries will finally deliver me to death's front door.

His hold on me remains tight and unwavering.

I force my eyes open despite their swollen nature and settle my sights on the thing I'm pressed against. A creature resembling a man, the one I had laid my gaze on earlier. When I made the simple and careless mistake of faltering.

Chiseled jawline, pointed nose, thick and bushy eyebrows. If he were of my kind, he'd be attractive, but he's not. His blood is tainted. His demonic nature is prevalent in the glowing red orbs of his eyes and pulsing energy he exudes. A trait that hunters like myself are capable of seeing thanks to the additional lens we were gifted with when we became of age. It allows us an advantage in our hunts to find our targets with ease. A talent that I have refined these past few years to become the best possible assassin I could be.

I suck in a breath, choking on the copper-tasting liquid caked on the inside of my mouth and throat.

The thing holding me tilts his head down and peers into my eyes. "Sleep." His voice is solid, stern, penetrating. It's powerful and commanding and somehow has total control over me.

My dreams are filled with endless recollections of my failure playing on repeat. Each one of them ends the same, with me being captured by the enemy and tortured until my warrior body finally gives out.

Killing me quickly would be too much of a gift that they would never be willing to give me. No, they want it slow and agonizing. Their joy comes from inflicting pain on others and draining the lifeforce gradually from their victims.

At least, when I kill their kind, I'm swift and merciful, ending their lives before they know what hit them. My job is to eliminate, not drag the process out. I don't take pleasure in murdering them—I take it in protecting my kind and eliminating any threat they may bring.

Some would say those go hand in hand.

I don't kill for fun. I kill because I must. Because it's what I'm good at. Because it's the only way for us to survive.

I was never going to be one of those girls who stayed home and made children. Who coddled their babies and tended to their partner's needs. Don't get me wrong, it's probably an equally difficult job, it just wasn't what I was designed to do.

Not when danger was always one step away.

I made that decision at the ripe age of three when my birth mother was brutally slaughtered, and I hid like a coward under the floorboards of the shack we lived in. There was nothing she could do to protect me, and the same could be said the other way around. Our home was set on fire and the smoke had almost gotten to me by the time I crawled my way out and ran as fast as I could to the neighboring town.

I was a child, and at that moment, I knew all I needed to know about the brutalities of this world and what I must do to protect myself, and those around me.

I wouldn't take the same path as the other girls my age —no, I would spend every single day training to become a fearless hunter, because that was the only option I saw in my mind. I would not allow myself to succumb to that same fate. I would not be helpless and fall victim to the demon bringers and the vile creatures they unleashed on us.

I would make it my life's mission to vanquish every last one of them.

And now, here I fucking am, reliving an endless nightmare of all the things I did wrong to end up where I am today. Beaten, bloodied, and close to death with those I hate the most.

My entire body aches—dull and sharp all at once. I suck in a breath of the stale air and wiggle my fingers, then my toes.

Yep, I'm very much alive, despite how fucking terrible I feel. And being able to move just that little bit means I'm not completely broken beyond repair.

Not that it matters, I'll never make it out of here alive, not if these brutal beasts have anything to do with it.

The scent of beeswax and rosemary tickles my nose. A healing salve.

I blink a few times, adjusting my eyes to the dimly lit room I've been put in, but don't bother moving. Not yet. I must take things slow and assess my surroundings before acting too irrationally. Hightailing out of here is a given, but I must be smart about it. I'm in no condition to take on two demons, especially the one who refused to let me die in that building. If he wanted me here, it was for some twisted game, and I refuse to play into his hand. If my survival stands any chance, I have to be strategic.

I sigh and scan the space. Not like I have much of a future if I make it out alive anyway. Dravin and Parla will have my head for the mess I created. Not eliminating my targets and getting taken is a huge no-no, along with the handful of casualties and weapons that were lost. I'm valuable to them, and they would rather I die at their hands than that of a demon. If my soul is captured by anyone other than the committee, it will mean an entire shitstorm for my people.

My essence is too precious for anyone other than the right people to get their hands on.

That's the thing with us warriors—our souls become more powerful with each demon life we end, their power diminishing and transferring over to us. There's more magic behind it than I'll ever begin to understand, but the moral of the story is—don't get caught. Not everyone knows this fancy little detail, but those that do are incredibly dangerous. Consuming a seasoned warrior's soul can do irreparable damage to what we've spent centuries working toward.

I should have died back in that building, alone, with no one around, and my soul to vanish into the abyss, never to be used as a power source by any other living creature. Instead, I'm here, going to die at the hands of the very man I was set out to kill.

Man…I shouldn't even refer to him that way. He's part man, part demon. A walking disgrace and a reminder of the life I lost all those years ago. He may not be directly responsible for my mother's death, but he might as well have shoved his fist into her chest and ripped her heart out himself. I can't look at a single demon without imagining it being them that ended her that fateful day. Or think that maybe they're the reason my father never came home. I never learned what happened to him, but I can only assume his death was caused by the evil creatures I wish to rid from our realm.

"You're awake," a soft voice says.

My heart goes wild, but I do my best to calm it. I will not lose control, not yet.

"Here." He stands from his spot in the corner and brings over a small cup.

How did I not notice he was sitting over there? I can smell the demon in the other room, but nothing of this one. No, he smells of cedar and lavender mixed with sweat.

I grip at the small cot I'm lying on and shove myself to where I'm sitting upright. My head spins and I continue to blink to clear my sights. I'm dizzier than I should be. Like there's a poison in my veins rendering me weak and unable to act normally.

My gaze settles on my left leg, and the two wooden

slats on both sides. Dirty fabric is tied around the top and bottom, securing it in place.

Why would they try to help me when they're only going to end my life eventually?

"Here," he says again. "Drink."

I lift a shaky hand and take the offering from him, watching his bright eyes shine through the murky room. I tilt it sideways and dump the contents on the floor, not caring about it splattering onto his shoes.

There's no way in hell I'd consume whatever that was and he's a fool for ever thinking I would.

"Ah, man. Really?" He snatches the cup from me, but instead of getting mad and hitting me like I expect, he walks back over to the small table with the pitcher and pours more of the liquid into the cup. "I get it, really, I do. You don't trust easily. But listen…" He steps over and kneels beside me, tipping the thing up to his lips. "Look." He takes a sip and swallows. "See."

I narrow my gaze at him, desperately trying to sense his aura. It doesn't add up. There's nothing demonic about him. He's also not one of me. And if that's the case, that means he's…human? We don't have those here though. Not in this realm. It's incredibly uncommon, if not rare for that to happen. The realms were closed off ages ago, and the chances of their kind surviving here are slim to none.

There's no possible way he could have made it through on his own.

I shouldn't, but I open my mouth anyway. "What are you?"

He continues to extend his hand, offering me the cup. "I'm Dash."

"What's a *dash*?"

"No, that's my name." He sighs and glances at the cup. "You should really drink this. You'll heal quicker if you do."

Why does he care if I heal or not?

I study his frame, sizing him up to determine whether I could overpower him in my current state. I've taken down larger beasts, telling me that the chances here are likely, but not knowing what waits for me outside this small room has me hesitant on acting just yet. I must be smart, cautious, mindful. All the things I was not when I hesitated and messed things up terribly.

"Why?" I eye the cup and then him.

His features are soft, not at all like the hardened exterior of the *thing* that carried me to my confinement. Thick, red hair, and kind eyes. Which can only mean he's good at this whole pretending to care act he's putting on.

Maybe they're going for the good guy bad guy thing to fuck with my head.

"Well, staying hydrated is important, obviously," Dash says. "And if you don't take care of your body, it will hinder its ability to bounce back from situations such as these."

Is he really explaining to me the importance of water? "That's not what I meant."

"What then?" He tilts his head slightly, a genuine confusion settling onto his handsome face.

"Nothing." I take the cup from him because regardless of his intentions, he's telling the truth. I need whatever strength I can recoup if I stand any chance of breaking free of my captors.

"Don't drink it so—"

But it's too late, I down it all in three swigs, a bit of the liquid trickling down onto my tattered but still intact armor.

My stomach immediately gurgles but I ignore it and assess the rest of my body.

I should be worse off than this. I was close to death when they took me, but now, I'm somehow remotely healed of a handful of the injuries I had obtained. That doesn't make any sense. None of this does. Why am I not already dead?

The door to the room bursts open and I do my best not to flinch at the sudden arrival. Instinctually, I reach for a weapon, but come up empty-handed. I grab the cup I had sat beside me and grip it in my hand. Anything can be a weapon if you try hard enough.

The intruder scoffs. "What do you intend on doing with that?" He leans into the doorframe and crosses his arms over his chest. His muscles bulge the dark fabric of the shirt he's wearing. He's more man than a beast at this point, but I can still sense his demonic nature.

I clench my jaw and imagine the many things I'd like to do to him. All of them ending in his death.

That's what I've trained for my entire life. Kill the demons and their bringers that have corrupted our realm with their impure and ruthless bloodline.

Many, many years ago, our realm was compromised by the demon bringers. A portal to the hell dimensions was opened and their kind was brought over to feast on the souls of all that called Prania their home.

A war ensued that went on for ages—finally resulting in triumph over the demons. The portals were closed off permanently, allowing no travel to and from our realm to any other. All that remained of their kind went into hiding, only to come out every so often to feast on the innocent when the opportunity presented itself. The more they consumed, the more powerful they became.

It is up to those with specialized skills like me to eradicate them before they can gain enough power to reopen another portal and unleash havoc on our realm once again.

Each of my kind they kill, the greater the chances of that happening. Especially when our power from killing them is transferred over if they consume our soul.

I cannot permit that to happen.

Another door opens, from outside this room. The man in the doorway flits his gaze at the source of the sound but remains firmly planted a few feet away from me.

I smell the thing immediately—the demon's heavy aroma filling the air at a quick pace.

His blood must be entirely made up of darkness if his scent is that potent.

Now there are three of them I must overpower if I intend to make it out of here.

It's not an impossible task, but my injuries will make it a difficult and interesting one.

"You brought a fucking hunter here?" The monster growls and tries to push past the other demon in the doorway. "Let me in there, I'll rip its flesh off and savor every last bite."

Yeah, it's safe to say things are about to get even more interesting.

2

BO

I hate hunters.

Warriors.

Assassins.

Demon slayers.

Whatever the fuck you want to call them, they're all garbage and I'd like to end every single one of them.

Preferably slowly, and as painfully as possible. You get what I'm putting down, right?

They kill us and I kill them.

I shove Wes and grip at his arm, trying to pry him out of my way. "What the fuck is wrong with you?"

He stands there, taking up the space and not budging to let me through. "Bocephus."

"You're really pissing me off, Wes."

"What's new?" He slams his hand into my shoulder and knocks me back. "A minute of your time before you dismember our newest arrival?"

I breathe in deeply and exhale, steadying my gaze on him. "Fine." I crane my neck to look past him. "How come Dash gets to be in there?"

Wes runs his fingers over his jaw. "Because Dash is harmless." He pokes me. "You, on the other hand, need to learn a little restraint."

I throw my hands up and take a step back. If they want restraint, they'll get it. For now.

"Sit." Wes points at our eating table in the front room.

I comply, only because I know if I give him a bit of what he wants, it'll get me closer to ripping that hunter apart with my razor-sharp teeth. Oh, what a tasty snack it will be.

"Wipe that murderous look off your face, too, while you're at it." Wes crosses his arms over his chest.

"What, is it your new plaything or something?"

"*She* could be the leverage we need."

"*She*?" I stiffen and glance toward where we just came from. I didn't notice *what* it was, only that it was the enemy. There aren't many female hunters, and in my time spent in this realm, I've only encountered one other. I didn't get the privilege of ending it, but she died that day all the same. One less hunter is a win in my book.

And considering there's one sitting in the other room, it's only a matter of moments before I end its life, too. *Her* life.

"Your ass stays firmly planted in that chair if you

know what's good for you." Wes draws my attention back to his stupid face.

"You better get to that part where you explain what's going on or I'm going to go in there and finish it off." My skin crawls at the idea of it being in such close proximity and not being able to wrap my hands around its throat until the life leaves its body.

They all deserve to die, especially the one in the other room. I can smell the stench of her kills lingering from her body despite her feeble attempt to cover them with magic. When you've been around as long as I have, those tricks no longer have the same impact they do on others.

"You want her back, don't you?"

At this, he steals my attention fully. "What kind of question is that? You know I do."

"Then let's use her."

"How?" She'll kill us the second she gets the chance.

"She's skilled, potentially the fiercest hunter I've come across in all my years." It's almost like Wes is bragging about her.

"Your point?" Because all he's doing is making me want to end her life even more.

"Her life is of value to them. We can barter her, get our people back."

I sigh and rub my temple. "That will never work."

Wes slams his fist on the table, splintering the weak wood surface. "Damn it, it has to."

I study his face, wondering why he's so hellbent on

doing the impossible. It's hard enough to survive, let alone go against their kind in the way he's speaking. Going directly to them is suicide, and it has been for everyone with demon blood who's remotely tried it. Prania is ruled and governed by *them* and only them. They answer to no one, especially our kind. We'll be executed on the spot, and that's if we make it there without being killed.

"Why her, Wes? What's different about her than any other hunter we've encountered?"

Wes shifts in his seat, a tell that he's hiding something. We all are, but for once, it's something new I'm unfamiliar with.

"Spit it out." The beast in me stirs, wanting to end this conversation and drain the hunter of its lifeforce, ridding her of any opportunity to kill a demon ever again.

"It's nothing," Wes lies. "Nothing other than the break we've been waiting for. A possibility we didn't think we'd ever get."

"It's never going to work. It's been years, Wes. The chances of them—"

He cuts me off. "Don't talk like that."

"What? For being realistic in managing my expectations? Something you're clearly unable to do." I clench my fist and dig my nails into my palm. The pain slices through me, my own venom stinging my skin. "And you think bringing a fucking hunter into our home is a good idea? You're going to get us all killed. Is that what you want?"

Wes lowers his head, and for a second, I almost feel sorry for him, but that's not an emotion I'm capable of feeling. "No."

"You have a week to figure this shit out, otherwise I'm gutting her." Oh, the satisfaction that would bring me.

Dash mutters something from the other room but I can't quite make it out.

The female appears in the doorway, and for a split second, I'm completely taken by surprise at her features. Dark hair spilling over her shoulders. Plush, pink lips that are cracked and swollen. A deep greenish purple bruise covering most of her face. Blood speckles her cheeks and somehow brings out the golden hue of her eyes. Her porcelain skin is dusted with dried remains of her injuries and potentially her victims. Thick armor covers her body and despite it being worse for wear, it hugs her like a well-fitted glove.

I've never seen a hunter so...

I shake my head. No. I will not allow myself to fall prey to whatever allure she exudes. She is the enemy, and she will remain that until I end her myself. But for now, I will give Wes the satisfaction of thinking he's in control of this situation.

Still, though, there's one thing I absolutely must do. And so, I stand, rushing across the space before anyone can stop me, and spin her toward me. Her scent mixes with mine, her frail figure weakened from the injuries she's still healing from.

I swipe at her hair, moving it from her shoulder, and sink my fangs into her flesh. Her blood pools into my mouth, a decadent flavor, more delicious than anything I've ever tasted.

She wiggles under my grasp, but I continue sucking and enjoying the heavenly surprise of her blood that gushes into my mouth and down my hungry throat.

A fire burns through the clothing covering my shoulder, and latches itself onto my skin in the shape of a hand. It's enough to send me back to reality, the one where Wes is screaming at me to stop, his radiant power melting the skin off my back while he pries this *female* from my grasp.

With her eyes closed, her body goes limp and falls into Dash's arms.

Wes shoves me with a force more powerful than anything he's used on me in the past. A rage unlike any other consuming him—something that makes no fucking sense at all.

She's just a hunter.

"What the fuck is wrong with you?" Wes growls, his other self partially showing through. His eyes glow fiery red. The hand he had touched me with, still a flame flickering along his skin. His own fangs exposed and ready to tear me apart.

I lean against the wall he pushed me into and wipe at my bottom lip with my thumb, licking the remains of her blood off it and allowing the high to consume me. "I was doing you a fucking favor."

"By sucking her dry?" His other fist ignites into a flame and his whole aura borderline engulfs, too.

When has he ever been this concerned about killing a hunter?

"No, you psychotic mutt. By *marking* her." I kick off the wall and point to her body, still being held by the pathetic human we keep around. "She gets too far away from me and that thing will go off like a beacon alerting every demon around to her presence."

"You put a fucking target on her back?" Wes's dark nature doesn't dim down at all.

"I mean, technically it was her neck, but yeah."

Wes acts quicker than I can react, gripping me around my throat and scorching me with his touch. "I'll show you a fucking mark."

"Guys, stop," Dash calls out from his spot hovering near the ground. Somehow, he stands, her body still in his grasp but now he's cradling her.

I've always thought he was a weakling, but he lifted her without wavering whatsoever.

He carries her body out of sight, back into the room she once was in.

Wes turns toward me and points his flaming finger. "You touch her again; I'll fucking kill you myself."

I roll my eyes. "I'd like to see that."

We're a similar height and stature—tall and wide, but with layers of muscle that allow us to crush our victims with ease. There's no telling whose beast is stronger, which makes me uncertain how I would fare if we went head-to-head. It's possible mine would crush his, but considering I've never seen his at full capacity, it's difficult to know with certainty. I might be a cocky shifter, but as much as I enjoy killing, I prefer to live, too. Still, I'd love for the chance to kick his ass.

"Don't test me, Bo." He growls low and shoves me one last time before leaving me there in the hallway.

If I didn't know better, I'd think he had feelings for this hunter, but I do, and there's no way he'd ever be stupid enough to care for the enemy. Either way, he's going to get us all killed with his foolishness.

3
WREN

I wake feeling worse than I did earlier.

My fingers skim the soft, raised spot on my neck. I wince and steady the anger that builds as I recall the cause of the new wound.

That fucking demon bit me.

"You going to run out of here again?" Dash quips from his spot in the corner.

I sit up and scoot myself against the wall. "Maybe." I swallow the dry lump in my throat and desperately wish for another cup of the water he had offered me earlier. And maybe something of substance to put in my stomach, and a healer to tend to my injuries.

I'd take my weapons, too. One to shove into each of their chests, straight through their hearts to end their lives with more grace than they intend on showing me.

"Are you thirsty?" Dash rubs his eyes and yawns.

"No."

"You're probably not hungry either, or in pain." He stands and walks to the door, turning once he's at the threshold. "Don't move."

And if I do?

Not that I intend on finding out, I'm too tired and worn out to protest. I must gain my strength if I'm going to make it out of here. I snuck past him once before, but the demon in the other room overpowered me with ease. There's no way I'd make it in my current weakened state.

In need of a stretch, I stand, doing my best to stay upright despite the brace on my leg and the dizziness that ensues from being vertical. I hurt everywhere but it will only get worse if I continue to sit still. There's no telling the damage my body has undertaken, especially now that I have demon venom laced in my veins.

I waddle over to where Dash was sitting and run my finger along the small table. Various herbs and salves are haphazardly placed about with no real order to any of them. I pick up one of the cylinders of brown mixture and bring it to my nose, inhaling the strangely familiar scent.

"Old family recipe." He hesitates and adds, "Not mine, but someone else's." Dash plucks it out of my hand and sets it on the table. "I thought I told you not to move."

I cautiously look him over while reading his energy. "I'm not much for following orders."

"Here." He raises his arm, revealing a banana held in his grasp. "Eat this."

Narrowing my gaze, I don't bother taking it.

Dash sighs and peels back the layers of the thing. He nibbles off a small section and holds it out toward me. "Now will you eat it?"

My stomach growls, giving away any chance I had at pretending I didn't want to eat.

"Why are you trying to feed me?" I carefully pluck the banana from his hand without touching him and hobble around to the other side of the table. I bite a chunk of it and force myself to savor the meal, uncertain when my next will be.

There's no telling what kind of torture they have in mind for me. The whole not knowing might possibly be the worst of all. I expected it to start already—either by way of beatings or some kind of physical abuse. Waterboarding, branding, asphyxiation. Maybe they're going for a slow, agonizing, psychological torment. If I'm being honest, I think I prefer the former. It's more predictable and easier to navigate. Whatever is happening now, I'm at a complete fucking loss.

"You won't heal if you don't eat," Dash says very matter-of-factly.

I swallow the mouthful and side-eye him. "And why does it matter if I'm healed?"

He starts to speak but is cut off by a figure appearing in the doorway.

My body tenses immediately, my hunter nature

sensing the threat all too late. My injuries are weakening me from the most basic of my skills and that alone is going to guarantee my demise.

"Fraternizing with the enemy, I see." It's the man-beast that brought me here.

"She needs her strength," Dash tells him.

I can only imagine what for, given my history with these types of creatures.

Dash I'm unsure of, but the *thing* in the door, he's up to no good.

"I'm sure you've already noticed, but the bite on your neck." He points to his own skin. "Has infected you with demon's venom."

I continue to eat the rest of the banana Dash had given me and pretend I'm not bothered by what he has to say. It's nothing that a bit of rest won't rid from my system soon enough.

"And since Bo is an alpha."

Those six words halt my heart.

My eyes widen and I do everything in my power to remain calm. "You're lying."

"Why would I lie to you?"

I shift my gaze to the human in the room.

Dash nods gently, a sincereness about his gesture, almost like he feels sorry for what happened. "It's true."

"What is this, some sick fucking game to you?" I steady my body against the wall and frantically search for anything other than this banana peel to arm myself with.

The monster raises his hand out toward me, and although he's across the room, I shrink away from him.

"Don't touch me."

His jaw tenses and he exhales dramatically. "It doesn't have to be like this."

"Why don't you just kill me and get it over with?" I blurt out at them, hoping like hell one of them will take me up on the offer and not realize the weight my soul carries. If I've made it this far, maybe they're unaware of the power it yields.

"We're not going to *kill* you." Dash looks to my captor. "Wes, tell her we don't mean her harm."

"I wanted to end your life the second I sensed your presence." Someone approaches from behind Wes—my radar confirming it's the monster who marked me. He nudges Wes out of the way, trying to get around him.

Wes holds his place but allows him to step into my line of sight.

The creature is as tall as Wes, similar in build, but with a darker aura about him.

Pure evil, my intuition tells me.

Long black hair pulled partially back, matching onyx eyes, and a jawline that must have been carved by the angels before he was discarded into hell. He brushes his tongue against his teeth, exposing his fangs to me. A grin settles on his face like he knows exactly what he's doing. Taunting me.

"Enough, Bo." Wes elbows him in the chest. "You're not making this any easier."

"Easier?" I laugh. There is no humor in this moment, not with three of my enemies holding me captive, no doubt planning something particularly evil.

If only I had killed them first when I had the opportunity. I'll never make that mistake again. I sealed my own fate when I faltered. I allowed *something* to distract me. Something I'll never quite make sense of no matter how many times I run it through my head. A strange flutter that filled my chest—a stirring, like something was awakening within me. A pointless nothing that would no doubt get me killed by the *thing* that caused it.

Now, I look at that same face that sparked that feeling and am struck with the realization that I was mistaken.

He side-eyes Bo and speaks. "You're not getting inside this room, not after what you did. So stop fucking trying to push past me." A guttural growl escapes him. "You cannot overpower me."

Dash slowly approaches me, a small cup in his hand. "Here."

I don't take my gaze off the men in the doorway as I slide the cup from Dash's hand and down the contents. I shouldn't trust him this easily, but he's given me no reason not to—other than aiding in my captivity. At every possible opportunity, he's shown me kindness and maybe if I play into that, I can use him to get free of these other two.

"Thanks," I tell him.

Dash points toward the bed. "You should sit, elevate that leg." He snaps his fingers like he suddenly remembered something and turns toward the table filled with various concoctions.

I watch him out of my peripheral while I continue to stare at the beasts in the doorway.

In my current condition, there's no way I could fight either of them, let alone both. Especially knowing that Bo is an alpha. That means his powers are stronger than I anticipated, possibly the fiercest demon I've come across. And here he is, having marked me and standing only a few feet away, practically foaming at the mouth to finish me off.

Legends say that being marked by an alpha is a surefire way to get killed, because the only way for it to not send out a glaring beacon to other demons, is to stay close to the one who bit you. But when the one who bit you is the sick fuck who wants you dead, there is no making it out alive. His venom might not kill me, but he will. And if I manage to get away, any demon within the surrounding villages will be on my ass the second I break free.

Maybe that's a reality I'll have to accept—that a target will forever be on my head, or well, neck. I guess it'll make my job easier, the demons coming to me instead of me having to go to them. Not knowing which targets are coming my way though, sure does complicate things.

I typically try to be thorough with my research,

figure out my enemy's strengths and weaknesses before going after them. It's one of the things that ensure my success rate. On rare occasions I hunt on a whim, it's usually prompted by a short notice order given by my authorities.

This last mission confirms my dislike of not being prepared.

I will do what I do best and figure my way out of this, though. I will strategize and use any resource I can to free myself, even if I have to start with the sweet red-headed human fumbling through the miscellaneous vials.

"Ah, there it is." He plucks a small dark-colored bottle and pours some of the contents into the cap. "Drink this."

What's with him constantly trying to feed me things?

Without asking, he sips a tiny amount and refills it. "Not trying to poison you. It's a healing tonic to speed up your natural healing process."

I make note of the way the bottle looks for future reference. I'll down the whole thing if it means getting better sooner and regaining my strength. I'd love to try my hand at fighting these two beasts and adding them to the souls I've consumed to rid them from this realm.

An alpha would no doubt fuel me in a way I could never imagine, making me an unstoppable force in the face of my enemies. Maybe then I could eliminate the filth from our world and give my people a fighting chance at truly being free.

Dash plucks the empty cap from my hand and secures it back on the bottle, tucking it in with the others it was surrounded with. He smirks, a bit pleased with himself—either from not having to convince me to consume the liquid or at having come up with the idea of the use of the tonic.

"Are you going to tell her, or shall we stand around all day gawking at the revolting bitch?" Bo leans against what little of the doorframe that Wes allows him to have.

"Language," Wes snaps at him.

Bo exhales dramatically. "She is rather revolting, there's no denying that."

I glare at him and imagine ripping his tongue out and shoving it down his throat.

"Tell me what?" I settle onto the bed, scooting myself up to the wall and bringing my injured leg up onto the sad excuse of a mattress.

It could be worse, I remind myself.

My thoughts float through countless scenarios of what Wes could possibly say next, all of which end terribly for me. Regardless, if they're going to confide in me their plan, it could help me maneuver my way out of it. I won't deny them of that error in judgment. Their loss will be my gain.

"We'd like to discuss your release." Wes seems

uncomfortable with these words, giving away a falseness to them that I'm not sure he realizes he's exuding.

I snort, crossing my arms over my chest. The movement sends spikes of pain through my body that I choose to ignore. I'm covered in bruises and abrasions from head to toe, just rubbing my skin against my clothing is uncomfortable. "Go on."

Fat fucking chance they're going to free me, but I'll entertain whatever this is considering I have nothing else to do at the moment while my body rebounds from the brutal beating it took.

"We have people at Rock Bridge. You're going to help us get them. If you succeed, we go our separate ways." Wes continues to stiff-arm the doorway to disallow Bo from getting through.

An alpha being subdued is a strange sight to witness.

Wes is clearly the one in charge, but why? Shouldn't Bo be the one calling the shots? How did that power dynamic switch from what the natural order should be?

Unless...

I swallow and will my hunter nature to come to the surface and examine Wes for what type of demon he is. My skills fail me, unable to read through his tainted aura. He's a demon, there's no doubt about that, but if he's able to dominate an alpha, he must be something powerful.

Is that why my superiors tasked me to kill him?

I was told he was some low-level grunt, nothing

special. An easy target. All I got was his whereabouts and the order to kill on sight. No one warned me of the magnitude of his power. Only that he must be eliminated.

They withheld vital information. Details that absolutely should have been disclosed.

"Are you listening?" Wes snaps his fingers.

I bob my head up and down. "Yeah."

"Then what did I just say?" Wes clenches his jaw and huffs, clearly annoyed by my lack of paying attention.

It's not my fault this entire situation is incredibly distracting. Between my injuries, my captivity, the demon venom coursing through me, and the puzzle I've yet to solve, my mind is going wild at trying to focus on any one thing.

I stare at him, unable to form a proper response. Truthfully, I have no fucking clue what he said. It couldn't be more important than figuring out what kind of demon he is.

Bo shakes his head. "Bitch isn't even listening."

I'm on my feet in an instant, despite the two boards strapped around my leg hindering me from moving how I typically do. "Why don't you come in here and say that again?" I rush over but Dash quite literally dashes over and steps in front of me.

I breathe in his human scent and push up against his warm non-demonic body.

How could someone so...*innocent* be in cahoots with these two hellish creatures?

Wes holds Bo back from bursting into the room, his hands glowing red as they pierce Bo's flesh. "If I have to remind you one more fucking time about your language."

Bo snarls at him. "You'll what? Huh." Bo squirms under Wes's grip. "Get your fucking hands off me."

Wes breathes and a billow of smoke comes rolling out, fire trickles behind it, and nips at Bo's hardened face.

Bo winces and ducks from being struck again by the flame. "What the fuck, Wes?"

Fire ripples on Wes's hands and out his mouth. He could be a witch, but no, I'd be able to sense that. His nature is too demonic. Dragon shifter? No, those have been extinct for quite some time, and he shows no other features alluding to that.

I rack my brain for what other demons have this ability, coming up short every time I think I find a lead to follow.

What could he be? And why am I so hellbent on figuring it out? He's powerful, that's a given. But maybe if I discover what he is, I can unearth his weaknesses, too—getting me one step closer to freedom.

Bo is a demon, clear as day. His blood is purely evil, nothing else about him. He's an alpha of his kind, making him that much more of a threat. Alphas are usually immune to a plethora of the typical demon weaknesses—lamb's blood, sugar, angel's feathers. Alphas have few flaws, and they're usually personal to the beast. I was once told that an alpha's ultimate downfall is its heart. Like, they have one of those. At least, not in the capacity of loving a damn thing other than killing my kind.

Dash continues to guide me away from the two idiots at the door. "You really should rest." He pauses, his hands gripping my shoulders. "I don't know your name." His brows furrow with the loss of not knowing that one word. He peers down at me, waiting for some kind of response.

His recent kindness is the only reason I open my mouth. "Wren."

"Wren," he repeats, trying it out for himself. He grins. "I like that."

I ignore the sense of satisfaction I feel rush over me at his smile. My injuries and the demon venom must be messing with my system, making me susceptible to his charm.

"Wren," another person mutters.

I glance around Dash to see Wes finally let go of Bo. They both gawk at me like I just grew a horn out of my forehead.

"What?" I ask them.

Bo waves his hand at the smoke billowing from his melted flesh, but remains in place, not coming forward despite Wes no longer blocking his path.

I hobble over to the bed and plop onto the mattress.

The minimal exertion wasted almost every ounce of strength I had. I am no longer the strong and capable warrior I once was. I have been weakened, subdued, and poisoned—my power at an all-time low in the worst possible situation.

I want nothing more than to escape this hell, but how will I manage that if I can't even walk across the room without overexerting myself? Is it the injuries? The venom? A different infection in my body I'm unaware of? Has Dash been using his soft nature to lure me in and trick me into consuming something that would keep me weak?

"I said…" Wes clears his throat. "That if you help us, we can cure the marking."

I blink up at him, his words piercing through my soul.

Cure?

That's not possible. There is no such thing for an alpha bite, other than death itself.

"You're lying," I tell him.

"I'm not."

"Why would I believe you?"

"I give you my word." Wes stands firmly in place, like his serious nature will somehow convince me he's telling the truth.

"Your word means nothing to me." I narrow my gaze at him.

He shifts slightly, almost flinching at my declaration. "These people, they're important to us. You might not care about them, but I do, and I wouldn't risk their life on that."

I desperately try to read him, not just with my hunter skills, but with everything I have. If it weren't for his demonic nature, perhaps I'd feel sorry for him. He seems genuinely concerned about whoever it is he wants to rescue. Maybe he is being truthful about the cure. But if that's the case, why have I never heard of such a thing in all my years?

I bite at the inside of my lip and recall my earlier thoughts, of not being informed that Wes was anything other than the fierce creature he is, dominating an alpha with ease. If that major detail was so easily omitted, what else have I not been told? Is it possible there is a cure after all? And if that's the case, wouldn't I be a fool for not doing whatever I can to get it?

Even if that means going against every single instinct I have and teaming up with the things I hate the most.

4
WREN

No one has ever made it out of Rock Bridge alive. Demons are taken there, tortured for information of the whereabouts of others, and slaughtered once they are of no further use.

It's the worst place for a demon to go. Not that they deserve any special treatment considering their existence is a plague I wish to rid from our realm.

Some low-level demons might get put to work at other locations, but Rock Bridge is a death sentence for anyone with demon blood.

I keep those details to myself though, because if I confess that to the men holding me captive, I might never get that cure they're bartering with. If it even exists. On the off chance that it does, maybe if I actually help them, they'll sympathize and follow through with their end of the bargain. If I want to be free of the mark lighting me up like a beacon to other demonic creatures, I have to at least try.

Countless things are going against me here. The wounds on my body. The lack of proper hydration and nutrition. The stress and fatigue I've undertaken. The venom flowing in my veins. The broken leg. The concussion. The fact that Dravin and Parla are no doubt sending out a team to either recover my soul or chop my head off for failing a mission. The hotheaded demon who marked me and wants nothing more than to end my life in the same capacity I want to end his. The beast that is more powerful than his comrade, one I can't quite figure out. I could go on and on, the odds continually being stacked against me.

At least there's Dash—the thoughtful and kind human who doesn't fit in at all here. It's hard to hate him when he's as soft as he is. An anomaly to this sick and twisted world we live in. Trusting him is dangerous, but I use it to my advantage; the more I grow lax to his presence, the more I can learn about the situation to gain an upper hand.

"I brought you something to eat." Dash steps into the room with a plate in his grasp. Resting on top is a large chunk of bread and a few pieces of cheese. "I'm sorry it's not much, we haven't made a supply run in a while."

I wonder where they typically get their resources from, but I don't bother asking. I don't want to hear the stories of the villages they must ransack and pillage to fuel their demonic ways.

Despite my sudden distaste for his offering, I take it anyway knowing if I don't nourish my body, I won't get better.

I plop a slice of the cheese into my mouth and lean against the wall. "Thanks." I finish chewing before speaking again. "How did you end up with those two?" I point toward the doorway where at least one of them is keeping put around the corner. Their energy floats toward me and when I suck in a breath, I grow familiar with the darkness.

If I'm not mistaken, that would be Wes in the other room, not Bo. Bo's scent is more pungent.

Dash sits in the chair at the small table in the corner. "Well, there's not much to the story, really." He scratches at his chin. "I woke up in the forest to them poking me with a stick. I guess they both thought I was dead." Dash shrugs. "I have no memory prior to that. Not of my name, where I came from, my family, nothing."

I chew another bite of the cheese and wait for him to continue.

"I had no idea who they were, but they refused to leave me out there. They took me in, let me tag along with them in the hopes that I would regain my memory and find my way home. Days went by, then weeks turned into months, into years. I never did piece anything together, and by the time I realized I wouldn't, there was no point in separating from them. It's..." He glances toward the door. "Too dangerous out there for someone like me. I don't have any powers, I'm just...me."

Two demons adopting a human—what a strange thing to witness. If I hadn't heard the story directly from his mouth, I'm not sure I ever would have believed it. And even now, part of me still doubts the validity of it all. Demons are cruel, brutal, violent—why would they spare this meager person's life? Not to mention, the liability he is to them, the weakness and weight of having to fend for someone who cannot fend for himself.

And to think that it's Wes and Bo, an alpha and... something else much more powerful. They should have ripped apart Dash on sight, eaten his flesh, and desecrated his body in their natural demonic ways.

Dash continues, "They trained me in combat, so I'm not completely useless, but I still stand no chance with the creatures of this world. And despite their extensive help, we haven't met any others like me in all our time together."

"They tried to find your family?" Another detail that surprises me. Perhaps they were just doing what they could to get Dash out of their hair without feeling guilty about it.

Demons don't feel guilt.

"For a while, yes. It was a fruitless labor though. And a risky one. I finally insisted that we stop and accept the fact that I was forsaken, abandoned, or just plain alone, whatever you want to call it. No one was coming for me, and there was no one out there expecting me to come home."

"You have Wes and Bo, you're not alone." I suddenly find myself trying to ease his sadness.

Dash smiles without showing his teeth and nods. "Yeah, you're right."

Shuffling in the other room draws my attention, and not a few moments later, Wes appears in the door. I ignore the immediate stir in my chest at the sight of him, and shove it down and away. Is it a warning? My natural instincts telling me to choose fight or flight if I want to survive? Whatever that is, I cannot afford to allow it to distract me.

He leans against the doorframe; a post he typically holds each time he somewhat enters this space. He doesn't come inside but maintains a distance. Something about it sets me on edge.

Wes looks me straight in the eyes. "Have you had adequate time to think over my proposition?"

I'm not sure there are enough seconds that could tick by that would prepare me for making a deal with the enemy. Never in a million years did I think my life would squander to this, but here I am, at his mercy, an alpha marker on my neck and no way out.

A week ago, I was at my peak, slaughtering anyone who dared cross me. I was strong and powerful and feared. Now...well, now I feel like a damn fool.

"I have," I tell him.

"And?" Wes stands straight, crossing his arms over his chest. His face hardens in anticipation.

"You're sure there's a cure?" I ask him, despite knowing he could lie to me.

Wes nods. "Yes. On my life."

Something I'm not so sure he realizes I don't care much for.

That unfamiliar thing in my core flutters again at that thought. Something inside me does not agree with my mind. So that's not a warning sign after all? Or maybe it's letting me know that I need him alive if I stand a chance. He does seem to be the only thing holding Bo at bay from ripping out my throat. And in my weakened state, I sort of need that assistance. I've got Dash on my side, what's the harm of doing the same with Wes until I can come up with an actual plan to break free. Even if they get me a cure, there's no telling if they'll follow through with letting me go. Hell, I wouldn't if I were them. I'd kill me on the spot before I had a chance to kill them.

"Okay."

"Okay?" Wes drops his arms to the side and hesitantly inches forward.

I sense Dash's gaze flitting between the both of us.

Wes takes a few steps into the room, closing that barrier of distance between us. He extends his hand. "Then it's a deal?"

I stand and hobble toward the beast towering over

me. His outstretched hand is massive compared to mine, and yet, I grip it anyway and firmly shake it, fully ignoring the strange sensation now coursing through me.

I've only ever touched a demon either during or right after I killed them. Never casually and this...intimately. What I expected to be repulsive and degrading, felt nothing different than that of shaking the hand of an associate. And like I already noted, aside from his aura, he appears similar to that of a man.

A rather attractive one, a little voice in my head tells me.

I push that ridiculous idea away.

"Can we have a moment alone?" He asks me while still touching me.

My mouth parts slightly, his request catching me off guard. "Um."

"I wish you no harm," he assures me. Glancing over his shoulder, he looks to Dash. "I don't need long."

Dash sighs and stands from his spot at the table. "You better not hurt her."

"What good would that do me?" Wes mutters before turning toward me. "Sit."

I do so without argument, surprising myself at how obedient I was to such a creature. Is that part of his gimmick? Mind control? That can't be true, otherwise, Bo would have been more receptive to Wes's commands without Wes needing to use brute force. Unless Bo can break free of the compulsion because of his alpha abilities. The variables are seemingly endless.

Wes kneels in front of me and studies my boarded-up leg. He hovers his hand just along the surface and shifts his attention up at me. "May I?"

I swallow and reposition myself. "What are you going to do?"

"I wish you no harm."

"You said that already, but that doesn't answer my question." My heart steadily gallops a bit more intensely at how close he is to my body. I do a quick scan of the room, my instincts trying to locate a weapon. I could rip the sheets off this bed, wrap them around his throat and choke him to death. Smother him with the thin and sad excuse for a pillow I've been using. Or perhaps rip one of the boards from my leg and smack him over the head with it.

A strong part of me runs numerous scenarios through my head, but a little voice floats in and tells me to do the impossible—trust him.

"I'm going to help you." Wes stares up at me through his thick lashes.

"How? Why?"

He breathes in and exhales slowly. "Wren…"

The sound of my name on his lips is something… completely unexpected.

"Fine." What do I have to lose? I'm already at his mercy. He could easily end my life in the blink of an eye at this proximity and the current state of my body.

Wes averts his gaze to my leg and lowers his head to where it's only inches away. His lips move but I cannot make out the words he's muttering against my injury. Slowly, he brings one hand up to untie the fabric at the top of the contraption, and the other to gently hold onto my ankle.

My eyes remain on him the entire time.

A cooling sensation fills the area he's whispering to, followed by a warm rush.

He continues to remove the thing from my leg and discards it to the side. "This is going to be painful, but it won't last, okay?"

Is this it? The moment he ends it all? Why go through the trouble of putting on a show? Is he weirdly ritualistic?

Still, I nod approval. "Okay."

He speaks to my leg once more through the armor of my bottoms. A snap rings out and I stifle a groan that forces its way up my chest. He wasn't wrong—that was brutal, but he was telling the truth when he said it wouldn't last, because within a few seconds, the ache I've felt for days dissipates into a dull and tolerable throb.

"How did you...?" I reach down and run my hands over my leg, wincing at how tender it remains to the touch but reveling in the no longer broken bone.

Does that explain why I am healed of most of the ailments I sustained? That it wasn't my body that did the repairs, but this beast before me?

Wes hesitates with his hand still resting on my lower thigh, almost like he's trying to make sense of the whole situation himself. He stands and dusts off his sides despite having nothing there to swipe away.

Is he nervous? Embarrassed? What strange behavior is this that he's displaying and why can't I figure it out?

He reaches for me. "Try to apply some weight to it."

I pause, too, but decide to take him up on his offer. I slide my hand into his and permit him to assist me in getting vertical. Cautiously, I maintain the majority of my weight on the other side, while slowly testing out the renewed limb.

Wes keeps his grip on me, watching me attentively.

I stand straighter as I challenge my leg to do its job. When it succeeds, I let go of him and take a step, then another. A few moments prior I could barely walk without being in pain, and now...I'm practically my old self. "This is incredible."

Wes grins. "Take it easy, killer. It's not fully—"

One too many steps in, a blip of discomfort shocks me, twisting my ankle and sending me falling face-first into...

Wes stops me from hitting the ground, my body landing smack dab into his chest. He softens the blow and wraps his arms around me, lifting me from the floor and into his arms. My mind is taken back to when he carried me to this place, my beaten and bloody body limp in his arms. I thought I was a goner then. Hell, maybe I still am. His breath is warm against my face, as is his frame pressed against my side.

"I'm fine."

Wes gently lays me onto the small bed and steps away. "I should have warned you; these things take time."

"Everything okay in here?" Dash pokes his head into the room. He frowns and steps inside. "What did you do to her leg?"

I scoot off the side, lowering my legs to rest against the floor of this small room. "He fixed it." I glance up at Wes, a bit of pink floating to the surface of his cheeks.

"It was nothing, I just set it in place." Wes rubs his neck and for a split second, I see him not as the beast that he is, but the humble man who showed me a gentle kindness.

It's only a moment before I realize it's for his own selfish reasons. He didn't offer me aid until he was sure that I would help him with his plan to rescue the other demons from Rock Bridge. An impossible task but if anyone could pull it off, it would be me. That is if they're not already dead. The likelihood of that being extremely high given the way history typically plays out. I've never heard of a single demon ever making it longer than a week in that place, let alone however long his kind has been there.

I've also never known of a demon to go to such lengths for another. They're typically lone creatures, not often teaming up with any outside their species.

These three are not only a complete abnormality, but the fact that they're going after others, that's unheard of.

Are those that they're attempting to rescue family? Friends? Part of their pack? Perhaps lovers? Or maybe they're powerful demons who can aid in reigniting the war that was over a long time ago. No matter the answer, I cannot allow them to fully succeed. I will do my part to get the cure, but then, I will have to end all their lives. That's the only way to ensure the safety of this world.

For now, I will play along.

5
WES

"What the fuck is wrong with you?" Bo throws a rock at me, but I catch it and drop it to the ground.

"Nothing. Why don't you fuck off?"

We continue through the woods, carrying the meager supplies we were able to acquire on a quick run. It's becoming more difficult for us to scavenge without drawing attention from hunters. The fewer of us that there are in existence, the more targeted their searches are for us. Every step we take is a glaring signal of our whereabouts.

Just like the mark that's lighting up Wren's neck.

My inner beast stirs at the anger of Bo's careless actions. I understand why he did it, but he could have at least consulted with me first. Not like Bo has ever done that in the past. I shouldn't have expected anything different now.

Bo had stayed within range of the cabin while I went out to gather provisions. He was close enough to hear a distress call but not far enough away that his distance would have activated Wren's marker.

Leaving her behind without protection was unsettling. Both because I wasn't there to provide it, and because I shouldn't feel that way at all.

She is a hunter. The worst kind of beast. She kills without regard and is the reason my kind has gone nearly extinct in this realm. According to rumors, I'm the last one standing, not only making me more powerful than an alpha, but of all alphas combined. It also makes the bounty on my head incredibly high. Prior to Prania being shut off from the other realms, my species was already diminishing in numbers. I wouldn't at all be surprised to find that I am alone in this world.

Perhaps that's why I relate to Dash and his situation. He's in our realm when he should be on earth with the rest of his kind. He is human. A mere mortal who has no recollection of who he is, or where he came from. There is no hope for either of us, given escaping this realm is impossible. We are doomed with a fate of fighting for our lives until we finally meet our end. Some days that reality is harder to stomach than others.

"What, are you attracted to her or something?" Bo continues to pry when he should keep his mouth shut.

Again, an unrealistic expectation for such a foul-mouthed bastard.

"That would be blasphemy," I tell him, because it's fully the truth.

A hunter and a demon. There could be no such thing. And yet, that doesn't stop my inner self from nearly bursting through the surface every time he catches a whiff of her scent. He wants her, and there's nearly nothing I can do to stop him. I am abundantly full of strength, but it is thanks to him, and he makes sure to remind me of that every second I spend denying his desire. I've never had to fight harder at withstanding his pull and I grow weary of how much longer I can keep his animalistic instincts at bay. His lust for her is misplaced, unnatural, and surely going to get us all killed.

Hell, it's the reason she's alive right now. If it were any other hunter, he would have let her die. I would have let her die. But the second I locked eyes with her, it was like I awoke from a lifetime slumber and fresh air was breathed into my lungs. I couldn't leave her there, not to bleed out and fade into nothing. No, I had to save her, and part of me is unsure whether that was me or my beast who made that decision. Perhaps it was both of us in tandem.

Something I will never admit out loud, especially to Bo. He'd never understand. Not when the only thing on his mind is killing anything that remotely smells of hunter. The fact that he showed restraint when marking her was baffling on its own. I was sure he would have drained her on the spot.

The second I saw her walk through that doorway, my heart nearly leaped from my chest. But upon seeing him grab hold of her and sink his fangs into her neck, I've never felt a rage quite like I did in that moment. I wanted to rip him apart. I wanted to end his life but in the most brutal way possible. How dare he think that he could touch her. He had been my partner for many years and despite our differences, up until that moment, I saw him as an equal. The second he laid a finger on her that completely changed. I had to restrain myself from killing him although the beast in me wanted nothing more. I could not give in to that temptation. But I did have to stop him.

I took great comfort in letting my beast rise to the surface and inflict pain on him. Although that fiery touch would have been nothing compared to the wrath he would've seen if he would've hurt her more seriously.

"It would be, yes. But that doesn't seem to be stopping you." Bo side steps a fallen log and continues along the path back to our sanctuary. The one spelled to repel hunters from pinpointing our location. It's not a permanent solution but it does the job for now. There's no telling how long until they find us and put an end to this incessant suffering of constantly being on edge and looking over our shoulders for the endless bitch that is our demise.

"You know nothing," I tell him.

"I know enough. And I'm no fool, Wes. You've got

the hots for the hunter." Bo laughs and adjusts the bag hung over his shoulder. "Not that I blame you, she is one fine specimen."

My beast reacts before I can, grabbing Bo by the neck and slamming him into a nearby tree. A fire ignites on my skin scorching everything that it touches, Bo included. "You will *not* talk about her that way."

Bo grins from ear to ear despite the flaming touch lighting him up. "Just admit it and I'll stop."

I clench my jaw and grip him tighter. "I will do no such thing."

His flesh bubbles under my touch. My other self begs to turn the heat up, but I keep it at bay. I don't wish to kill him. Not yet, at least. My beast on the other hand wants to end him for speaking of her.

Bo shrugs. "Then neither will I."

"I could kill you right here, right now." I squeeze his neck.

"You won't." He continues to smile through the torment of my touch. "You need me."

"I need no one."

"Keep telling yourself that."

My senses alert me to a sound in the close distance. I focus my attention on it, a momentary distraction that Bo uses to his advantage as he frees himself from my hold and punches me across the face.

I bring my flameless but smoking hand to my cheek. "You fucking asshole."

"Oh, I'm the bad guy? You're the one unleashing

your fucking beast on me." He picks up the bags and storms off, not saying another word the rest of the way.

We arrive at the cabin and I outstretch my arm to stop him. I pause to listen to her laughter float through the space and out to my ear, a soothing lullaby to my aching soul. How completely fucking wrong of me to get relief from such a thing.

Bo shoves me off him. "I won't hurt your precious hunter." He glances over his shoulder on his way up the small porch. "But that doesn't mean I won't eye fuck her."

My beast lets out a growl, my entire body engulfing into a roaring fire that I quickly disengage. "Simmer down," I tell it. "You're being irrational."

Another groan bubbles out of my chest as if to challenge my command.

I suck in a deep breath and ground myself. "She is not yours; you need to realize that. The sooner you do, the easier this will all be."

My beast stirs, my heart aching with the words I spoke. It pains us both, but the truth of the matter is, she is a hunter. She is a means to an end. She will only be around long enough to serve her purpose and then we will go our separate ways, so long as she doesn't go against her word and kill all of us first.

It's not what I want; it's not what my beast wants, but it's what must be done.

I waste no more time stewing in the yard and follow Bo into the small place we currently call home. It's not much. A one-bedroom shack hidden in the thick of the forest with an outdoor bathroom. There's a stream close enough for us to gather water from, that of which we must boil over the fire if we intend on bathing. It wasn't always like this. We once lived like royalty, with running water and ample food sources. But now we are fugitives in a land we cannot escape, fighting for our lives every single day. It's only a matter of time until we are caught but until then I will do everything in my power to stay alive. My beast does not give in easily and neither do I.

I step across the creaky threshold and into the front room that also triples as our kitchen and dining room. Two small couches line both walls in the corner. The place where we sleep when given the chance. We used to take turns, or well, fight over the bedroom, but with Wren here, it's only obvious to allow her to stay in there. And with no window attached, unless she got wickedly creative, there's no way for her to escape without us realizing.

My beast tugs me toward her, demanding that I get closer and at least confirm she is still okay. I hate how helpless I feel as his longing for her seeps its way into my own soul. It's difficult to differentiate where the origin of the desire comes from when I want her just as badly. Of all the females he could have taken a liking to he had to choose the worst possible one. Why are we both equally as fucking stupid? To yearn for a woman we can never have.

Says you, my beast taunts. *She will be mine.*

"Shut up," I blurt out loud.

Bo tosses the empty bag onto the floor and glares at me. "I didn't say anything."

For once, he actually did have his mouth shut.

"Not you." I run my hands through my hair. How am I going to go along with this plan when my beast is so unruly?

Bo sighs and crosses his arms. "That mutt trying to overpower you?"

"I don't need your smart-ass mouth, Bo." What I need is to see her and reassure my disobedient beast that she hasn't disappeared.

Isn't her scent alone enough? Or the sensation of her near proximity? Clearly, he can tell she's near the same way I can. But that's not sufficient for such a greedy creature. He's not used to being told he can't have something. He takes what he wants, when he wants. Perhaps denying him is only fueling his desire that much more. Maybe if I satiate those cravings he will calm the fuck down.

I go the rest of the way into the house and step into the doorway. I maintain my distance, afraid that if I give him too much, he will overpower me and claim her fully. He's already made it clear that she will be his, but if he marks her, similar to what Bo did, there's no stopping him from following her wherever she may go. I cannot allow him that authority. Not when being with her would only get us killed.

I risked too much when I offered to heal her. It's one thing to mend her wounds when she's unconscious, but feeling her golden stare on me while awake, it was a dangerous thing to do. When she fell, I considered letting her fall to the floor just to not touch her and give him the satisfaction. I couldn't though—my own pull to her overrode that rational thought and swept in to whisk her to safety.

I should hate her. I want to hate her. But it's something I find myself unable to do.

She stiffens when I arrive, the carelessness she exudes when in Dash's presence alone being replaced by the hatred she no doubt feels toward me. I don't blame her. She was born and raised with a delusional mindset that anyone with demon blood was the enemy. She was taught to hate us, to want us dead. Typically, the females of her kind are the homemakers, not the hunters. Which only reinforces the idea that she chose this path due to some heavy influence that caused her to hate us that much more. Whatever her reasoning, it still doesn't justify eradicating us completely from this realm. Some of us were just innocent bystanders caught up in the remnants of a war from long ago. Some of us are simply trying to survive until we can find a way out of this hell.

Have I killed my fair share of hunters? Absolutely. But I did so because I had to. It was me or them, the choice a simple one. It goes without saying that I have ended the same number, if not more, of demon lives with the exact reasoning. As with any species, there are bad apples. And with each of them waging a war against one another, it's only natural they would have an immense hatred for each other. I once called Prania home, but I wish to rid myself of this realm and find refuge elsewhere and perhaps live a life where I am not constantly fearing whether I would see the light of the next day.

I won't do so until we get our people back though. I've been searching for countless years for a way out for me and my own, only to have that halted when a ruthless hunter broke us apart. Each passing day, the chance of getting them back dwindled, but when my beast locked its sights on Wren, I felt that flicker of hope reignite in my soul. Perhaps we could both get what we wanted after all. Him, a chance to be near her, and me, the return of my people. *Our* people. Me and Bo. We both lost someone that day and I will stop at nothing to get them back, even if that means trusting the one who sees me as their enemy.

"Did you find what I was asking for?" Dash stands from his chair and walks toward me.

Wren scoots further away from me and leans against the farthest wall.

"I did." I tilt my head in the direction I came. "It's in the kitchen."

"Cool." He slaps my shoulder and steps around me. "Thanks, Wes."

Despite the small size of the house and the people

just in the other room, it dawns on me that she and I are now alone. A welcomed thing for my beast.

"You going to stand there and stare?" Wren mouths off.

My beast stirs at her feistiness and recalls watching her eliminate three demons with absolute ease prior to her locking her eyes on us. A feat not taken lightly given her size and stature. She is small but she is lethal. It was that momentary exchange that caused her to waver, allowing her enemy the upper hand. I watched in terror as six other demons descended upon her, attacking her from all directions. Something she might have been able to overcome had I not been there and forced her to stutter. I felt her soul the second I walked into that place. The sensation rattling through me was completely foreign and yet so fucking familiar. My beast had no doubts that she was the one.

I rose from my spot across that old, abandoned building and single-handedly ripped apart all but one of the creatures that took her down. I would have finished the last of them too, had Bo not chased him off and made a game out of hunting him.

"Maybe," I finally say. "Is that an issue?"

Wren blinks up at me like she's analyzing my every movement. "It's a bit creepy, if you ask me."

Go toward her, the voice in my head commands.

"Do you mind?" I point at the chair Dash typically sits in. Perhaps that will suffice both of us without giving in too much.

She narrows her gaze. "You're holding me captive, yet asking permission to sit in your own home?"

"Shall I take that as a no?" I continue to lean in the doorframe and study her as she does the same to me.

"By all means..." She motions for me to come inside.

I lower myself onto the stiff chair and rest my arm on the table, scanning the strewn about contents to avoid looking at her.

"Is there something I can help you with? Or are you just here for guard duty?"

I drag my gaze from the herbs and potions to meet hers. I stare for only a moment and somehow it feels like an eternity, my soul igniting with a blaze unlike anything I could have imagined. What is wrong with me? Why her? Of all the women in this realm, it had to be a hunter? Internally, I curse at my beast for choosing her over anyone else. *Fucking fool.*

"No, I..." I don't typically find myself at a loss for words. I may be a man of few of them, but this, this feeling of helplessness and confusion at the situation is overwhelming. "I thought we could discuss how to move forward." There we go, think logistics and strategy. That will be a nice distraction.

For you, not me, my beast scoffs.

She hesitates before nodding. "Yes, that would be wise." Wren scoots herself to the edge of the bed and reaches to pick up the cup on the floor. She brings it to her lips and drinks some of the water.

I don't mean to, but I watch her intensely as if every movement is a work of art.

I bite at the inside of my cheek, drawing blood and allowing the sensation to snap me out of my stupor. It's only mildly successful.

I can't stay away; my beast won't allow it. And I can't be near, otherwise my mind turns into a pile of fucking mush. How is it possible that I am quite literally the most commanding of my kind in this realm but in her presence, I am completely powerless? What a complete contradiction. And if she knew it...well, I'd be a goner no doubt.

"Well, then, what's the plan?" Wren sets the cup back in its place but remains on the edge of the mattress. Her still weakened body hanging over and calling mine toward her.

No, I will my other half to understand. *She would never want us; you need to get that through your thick skull.*

These thoughts and feelings are not mine alone.

He's right. I'm just as guilty for this absurd obsession as he is.

But it's not like I can back out now. I must follow through with this plan, otherwise Bo will never remove the mark and we may never rescue our people. It's best for us all if we get this done as soon as possible and go our separate ways.

I won't allow that, he growls.

You have to, we don't have another choice in the matter.

"Wes, hello?" Wren waves her dainty hand in the air. "Are you purposely ignoring me or what?"

"No, my apologies. I have quite a bit on my mind at the moment." I provide her with what little of the truth I can. After all, I cannot lie to her, not when my beast has set his sights on her. I'll have to get creative with the words I use so I don't give her too much of the upper hand. At the end of the day, she would still betray us given the chance and I will not permit my beast to put us in danger that way.

"Is everything all right?"

I'm surprised by her question, caught off guard by it, actually. So much that I do that thing where I just stare at her for far too long. I can only imagine how absolutely insane I must appear to be from her perspective.

Bo stomps into the room, his sudden appearance stealing both of our attention. He plops onto the bed next to Wren and leans against the wall. "Sup?"

She and I stand at the same time, stepping toward each other. I shove her behind me and steady the fiery rage coursing through me.

"Oh, chill out." Bo raises his hands in the air. "I'm only having a seat. Would you rather I take that one?" He points to the chair I was in. "And you can sit here." He pats the bed, a bit of dust scattering from the dirty blanket.

I'm not sure which is worse, having Bo close to her, or allowing my beast the pleasure of being that near. I can somewhat control both of them, but I'd rather take my chance with the internal idiot I've spent my entire life with.

I grip Wren's hand, taking note when she doesn't flinch or jerk away. Pulling her toward the bed, I smooth out the blanket and offer her a seat before settling in next to her. I keep my guard up and my beast at bay. He purrs with satisfaction at the close proximity.

"Now that you two love birds have settled in..." Bo leans into his chair and props his legs up on the table, crossing them and his arms behind his head.

I ignore his comment but not the slight shift that Wren makes.

Bo snatches a small splinter of wood from the table and picks his teeth with it. "Breckenridge will be our first stop. We leave in the morning."

Wren interjects immediately. "That's demon territory."

"Yeah, and we're demons. What's your point, Birdie?" Bo doesn't bother looking at her, instead he uses that same splinter to scrape under his nails.

"Birdie?"

"Mmhm. Thought of it myself. What do you think?" He's taunting her. He's taunting me. He's taunting my beast. And he's doing a damn good job at it.

I choose to disregard his attempt and focus on the task at hand. Tilting my head toward her, I explain. "It's a safe spot for our kind. That will be our first destination on our way to Rock Bridge."

"But I'm a hunter. They'll kill me on the spot."

Over my dead body, my beast growls.

A bit of his groan rumbles in my chest, giving away more than I'd prefer to show.

Bo laughs and plops his feet onto the floor. "Fucking told you."

"Told him what?" Wren looks between us, confusion furrowing her brow.

Her questioning cannot persist if I stand any chance of ignoring the truth. "The beacon on your neck will also provide a mask to hide your true identity. They will see you as one of them, not of the enemy."

She shakes her head. "I don't think you understand. I'm Furla Ain, people know who I am."

My chest tightens. I knew she was feared, but I had no idea she claimed this title.

Me, the most powerful demon—her, the deadliest demon assassin.

"Now that," Bo chuckles. "Is fucking hilarious."

Wren rises to her feet, advancing on Bo. She kicks him in the shin. "What, because I'm a girl? Because I'm small." She grabs blindly at the table, snatching a wooden spoon and holding it to Bo's neck. "I've ended bigger and stronger demons than you."

Bo smiles from ear to ear and steps into the thing at his throat, towering over her when he says, "Do it, then you'll be marked forever."

I shove myself between them, pushing their chests with my open palm to separate them. My skin brushes against hers, my beast salivating in response. I drop my hand from her body and look at the instigator. "Can you be serious for one fucking minute?"

He raises a brow. "Sure." Bo tilts his head around me to focus on Wren. "It's not because you're female at all. It's because Wes—"

I clench his throat and permit my powers to flow through and scorch his skin. Cutting off his airway and ability to speak, I thrust him into the wall and raise my arm until his rather large body is dangling above the floor. "Do you wish to die? Is that it?" I grip tighter, my touch melting his demonic flesh that had already been healed from my previous assault.

"Wes," a dainty voice calls at me from behind. She places her soft but calloused hand on my shoulder. "Let him go."

I drop Bo immediately, my beast submitting to her request. Oh the power she already has over me without even knowing it.

Bo clutches his neck and gasps for air. "Fuck, Wes. Are you out of your mind?"

When it comes to her, there's no denying that. Everything I've done since I laid my sights on her has been insane. And I can't imagine that that will change.

6

WREN

I shouldn't find it surprising that my captors are keeping secrets from me and yet I am growing incredibly curious about what it is that they are withholding. It's like some inside joke that they refuse to let me in on. It makes sense for them to have those, but it seems directly related to me and that detail alone makes me want to be in on it, too. Especially if it could be the difference of whether or not I make it out of here alive.

Wes is weirdly protective of me. I can sense his tension rise each time Bo is near. And considering Bo wants nothing more than to end my life, I can understand the threat that he poses. I am potentially the only chance they have of getting their people back—if they're not already dead. Wes wanting to keep me alive is the obvious choice if they want their plan to work.

But shouldn't Bo want the same?

Why is he so insistent on taunting the hell out of Wes in the process?

"Breckenridge." I tug at Wes to provide some kind of distance between the two of them.

He turns toward me, his eyes glowing red and his aura showing brighter than I've ever seen. It's almost...

No. I shake my head and rid myself of the thought. I will not allow his allure to consume me. He is a demon. A monster. The enemy.

As if noticing my mindset change, he blinks and the glow disappears, revealing a seemingly normal gaze.

"I didn't mean to frighten you." His demeanor softens.

Is that what he thinks that was? Fear? And if it was, why would it matter either way?

"You didn't," I assure him. There isn't much I'm afraid of anyway. I've pretty much seen the worst of the worst. Battled demons of all sorts. Ogres, Burners, Flapping Mitts, mutts from all the hell dimensions, shifters of many different variations, you name it, if it's lived in this realm, I've probably killed one or two if not more of them. I wouldn't be surprised if I'm the reason Bo ascended to alpha. Wes on the other hand, I'm still unsure what he is. I've yet to come across anything similar to him, convincing me that he may be the only one of his kind.

Is that even possible?

Would I have known about such an unusual species?

Shouldn't Dravin and Parla have warned me of such a thing?

Did they not have any knowledge of his rarity either? Or did they simply not tell me to keep it a secret. To keep others from finding out and potentially stealing his power source.

If his energy got into the wrong hands, it could be devastating to everything we've worked toward to regain control over our nation.

"You're a sick fuck." Bo's neck begins to heal before my eyes, his skin repairing itself and the charred remains littering the floor at his feet. He shifts his gaze to my leg. "You healed her leg, didn't you? Isn't it fucking obvious, Wes?"

What is he talking about?

"She would be of no use to us while injured, Bo. You know this."

A knock sounds at the door. "You two want to maybe stop acting like children?" Dash continues into the room, stopping right beside me. "You good?" His blue eyes look me over.

"Yeah." Leave it to the weakest in the space to be the most level headed.

"Are you interested in a shower? Surely you'd like to get clean prior to heading out tomorrow?"

Bathing hadn't even crossed my mind, but now that it has, my clothes suddenly become itchy and uncomfortable. I glance down at my dirt and blood-covered body, noting how terrible I must smell. "That would be preferable."

Perhaps freshening up will provide me with a renewed sense of self given the rather peculiar situation I've gotten myself wrapped up in.

Dash and I leave Bo and Wes behind to stew in their petty dispute. Whatever is going on between them is not a concern of mine. It's clear I'm involved somehow, but there's no sense in getting worked up about it if they refuse to tell me.

We step into the space that I had made it to when I had escaped the room I was being held captive in. It leads directly into a cluttered, open area with a small kitchen, a tiny table, and tattered couches. There are no other doors aside from the one leading to the porch and there is only a single window above the sink basin in the kitchen. I had thought I was being held in squalor, when in reality, they had given me the only bedroom in the house while they made do with the couches and hard floor of what they call their living room.

This is how they live? It's no wonder they're miserable.

When we reach the front door, Wes appears in a flash, slamming his hand into the thing to stop us from exiting. He looks directly at me. "Do not run."

I had no intentions of doing so, not knowing where I am or what would happen when I get too far away from Bo. He had gone out on a supply run and with each bit of distance he put between us, I could feel the mark growing warmer. I was told he wouldn't go far enough to set the beacon off, but even with that much space, the thing became uncomfortable to bear. It wasn't painful, just a reminder that I was no longer free to do as I wanted without consequence.

But even knowing I didn't intend on leaving, Wes's command solidifies that within me. Another sign that I am losing control over my free will. And to a freaking demon.

What has my life come to?

"She won't," Dash tells him, for me. "Now move your arm."

Wes huffs but ends up complying. He reaches for the knob and opens it for us. "Don't be long."

Wes is aware he has authority over me, because why else would he be comfortable in letting me go outside this place with a human who I could easily overpower and escape from?

In all my experience, I've never come across a demon who could possess such power over a hunter. Does that make me weak? Incompetent? A disgrace to my kind?

Dash guides me through the door, onto the dilapidated porch, and around the side of the shack they call home. The air is comfortable, not too warm, not too cold, but it's thick with fog and the lingering smoke from the surrounding villages that have been burnt to the ground.

Without drawing too much attention to myself I

skim the vicinity with my gaze, looking for any kind of identifying factor. Somehow, it all looks the same. Overgrown trees billowing with weeping greenery that fades into a shit-colored brown. Paths leading from each direction of the home show no clear sign of which way they come and go. There's no telling where we are, at least I've never been here before. But if Breckenridge is our first stop that must mean we're close to there. A location I don't venture often to, and perhaps the reason why they chose it, because I would be unfamiliar with the territory and the likelihood of me escaping would diminish considering the number of demons in a demon-infested area. Leaving their sight would be foolish of me given the glaring beacon on my neck that would attract every single demon around.

"I took the pleasure of heating the water for you." Dash points to the wood-slatted area.

I peek my head around the corner and study the outdoor shower. Dark stone covers the ground and vines twirl up and between the wooden walls. It might not be much, but it very well could be the nicest part of this thing they call home. If it weren't for the smog lining the air and the demons holding me captive, this wouldn't be an entirely unenjoyable experience.

Dash comes to my side. "That lever over there, just pull it down when you're undressed and ready. Don't tug it all the way, only slightly, and you'll have to do it every minute or so to keep it flowing. It's nothing special but you should get about ten minutes out of it.

There's soap down there." He grazes his hand against my lower back before exiting the space. "I'll be, uh, out here." He nods and closes the gate to the shower, leaving me alone in the decent-sized space.

I step in further and sit on my ass, reaching down to unbuckle my boots. I slide each of them off, setting them out of the way, and stand to unbutton my armored pants. The material is thick and clunky with various compartments for hidden weapons. Each of which has been robbed from my possession by my captors. Each time I graze an empty spot, a sigh of disappointment leaves me. How dare they be thorough at their jobs.

I peel my bottoms off, wincing at each unhealed wound still left on my body. I'm in rough shape, but nothing compared to a few days ago. I would have bled out on that dirt-covered floor had they not decided to spare me. Although, they may be only prolonging the inevitable. I drop my pants with my boots and go to work unbuckling my top. I pry it from my filth-covered body and revel in the weightlessness of not carrying the brunt of such armor. I feel exposed, vulnerable, but in the moment, completely free. As free as a captive person can be, given the circumstances.

Stepping out of my undergarments, I undress completely and turn toward the overhead contraption. I reach for the lever Dash had told me about, coming up short when I stand on my tiptoes.

Fuck. I guess that's what happens when you try to

wash in some seven-foot-something demon's shower. Dash is significantly shorter than Wes and Bo, but for a human, he's still exceedingly tall. Me, on the other hand, I was not blessed in the height department. Although, it has served me well in sneaking in and out of rather tight and confined locations.

"Um, Dash," I call out.

"Yes? Is everything okay?" Dash responds with a bit of concern lining his tone.

"I'm afraid I can't reach the lever." I stand taller and attempt one more time to no avail. "Can you get it for me?"

"You want me to...come into the shower with you?"

I yank open the door, revealing myself in nothing but my birthday suit. "Don't be modest. You've seen other naked women before."

Dash's mouth drops open. "Wren, you're...you're nude." He glances down for the quickest second and covers his eyes.

"Do you shower with your clothes on?" I ask him while tugging his arm and dragging him into the space with me.

"No, but I..."

I grip his shoulders and turn him so his back is to me and toward the lever I cannot reach. "There. Sorry, I didn't mean to offend you. I should have asked before exposing myself to you."

"I mean, I'm not mad about it." Dash reaches up and pulls the thing, the warm water beginning to flow down and trickling over my bare body. He steps out of the way of the stream but keeps his back to me. "It was unexpected is all."

"Such a gentleman." I run my right hand over my left arm and rub at the dried dirt and blood caking my skin. "Unlike your friends."

He nods. "They're not all bad. Well, Wes isn't. Bo is questionable."

By that I'm not at all surprised.

"Can you hand me that soap?" I close my eyes and submerge myself under the stream, soaking my hair in the process.

"Yeah, of course." Dash leans down to get it and reaches back to give it to me. "Does that hurt?"

I laugh. "Which one?"

He glances over his shoulder, a look of pity on his freckled face. "All of them?"

"A little, some more than others." I lather my hands and scrub at my face. The small cut on my lip reopens and blood from the wound trickles down my chin and mixes with the dirty water from my body. "Shit."

"You okay?" He tilts his head to the side but doesn't look.

"Nothing I can't handle."

I use the same soap for my hair that I do my body, but it works all the same, ridding most of the gunk from my dark locks. I snatch my belongings and bring them under the water with me. I give them a solid scrub, rinsing and tossing them over the side of the shower to air out while I make quick but effective work of cleaning myself the best I can given the accommodations. When I'm somewhat satisfied with my personal hygiene, I stand there, unmoving and allowing the water to crash over me. "I'm done."

Dash stands on his toes to look over the shower. "You have some water left if you want it."

"What about you? Do you need to bathe?"

He chuckles. "Are you implying that I stink?"

I shouldn't, but I place my damp hand on his shoulder. "No."

What the fuck am I doing? And why does it seem so wrong yet so right?

Dash's body stiffens and then relaxes. "Wren." My name is just a whisper on his lips.

In these few days, he's done nothing but try to make me feel comfortable despite my confinement. We've shared stories, laughs, and have broken bread together. He's attempted to gain my trust and has been an unlikely friend and companion. I'd be lying if I said I wasn't drawn to his innocence, his candor, his ordinary nature. No, that's a lie—Dash is not ordinary, he is a rarity to this world, perhaps more so than the alpha and unknown creature inside the very building this shower is attached to.

He turns around slowly, cautious with his gaze as he keeps it at eye level with mine. "Your lip..." Dash hovers his hand next to my face.

I lean into his inviting touch. "It's nothing."

Dash trails his fingers along my cheek and down my neck. He runs his thumb over my collarbone and rests his palm on my shoulder. "Wren, you owe me nothing."

"We're running out of water." I glance up at the slowed trickle of liquid.

Dash reaches to tug the lever and renew the stream, then immediately steps into it, pressing his mouth to mine and parting my lips with his tongue.

I moan against him and press my wet body to his clothed one.

His hands roam my frame, settling on my lower back and my neck. Dash tugs me into him and kisses me with a feverish intensity. "I..." He breaks away, his breath ragged. "I haven't been with a woman since..."

I stop my advancement and look him directly in the eyes. "I'm so sorry, I didn't mean to force myself on you. I thought—" I pause and shake my head. "I shouldn't have assumed."

Dash smiles. "No, trust me, I *want* to. You're the most beautiful woman I've ever laid my eyes on. It's just..." His expression changes. "I have no idea what I'm doing."

"We can stop." I wipe his dampened red hair off his brow. I don't want this to be a bad experience for him, even if it's my last chance to be intimate with a man before I trek across this forsaken land to a fate that will likely end in my demise.

"Do you want me?" He swallows in anticipation.

I nod. "I do." I latch onto the hem of his shirt and pull the thing over his head.

He grins again and melts his mouth onto mine, his hand wrapping around my waist and lifting me off the stone-covered ground.

I secure my legs around him, ignoring all the little aches and pains of the injuries still healing on my body. The pleasure of his touch is everything I need to distract myself from the overwhelming shit show that has consumed my life.

Dash presses my body against the wooden wall of the shower and continues to taste my tongue with his. With my leg still wrapped around him and my arms around his neck, he reaches down to undo his pants and drag them over his growing erection. "Are you sure?" he asks me.

I answer him by sliding my hand down and stroking his thick length.

Dash sighs and cups my breast, pinching my nipple between his fingers.

The water trickles onto us, keeping us from getting too cold as the temperature grows chillier in the approaching nighttime.

"I want you," he moans into my mouth.

I glide him into place and whimper when his cock penetrates my eager hole.

"Is that okay?" Dash fills me with caution, treating me far too delicately than he should.

"Yes. Is it okay for you?" I pivot my body up and

down the best I can from this position.

Dash exhales and smirks. "More than okay." He tightens his grip on my waist with one arm and extends the other to hold onto the shower wall. He's surprisingly strong despite being a meager human. He thrusts inside of me like he knows exactly what he's doing. His muscle memory doing him justice despite him having no recollection of being with a woman.

He skims my neck with his lips, sucking on my neck and biting the soft skin.

I tighten around him, my climax growing nearer sooner than I expected. I guess it's been a while since I've been intimate with another, too, and my desire for affection was higher than I realized. I don't get much downtime in my profession, leaving minimal opportunities for basic needs to be met. Plus, it's not often I'm held captive by three incredibly attractive men. If only two of them weren't the enemy, then things here could have gotten much more interesting.

Dash rests his forehead on mine but continues rocking his hips up and down. "Does that feel good?"

Something about his genuine consideration turns me on even more. "Yes," I moan.

He picks up his pace, slamming me into the shower wall. His hot breath floats across my shoulder, his teeth nipping the skin. "Fuck."

I come undone, my body spiraling into a whirlwind of pleasure and temporarily transporting me to somewhere far away from here, where it's only me and him, no demons, no other hunters, no obligations, or threat to our safety. All my pain is erased, and I become one with the pleasure.

"Wren, that was…"

"Put me down," I whisper into his mouth.

He gently lowers me to the shower floor, his cock gliding out of me in the process.

I grasp it in my hand, swirling my grip around his lust-soaked rod and stroking him.

Dash leans down, placing his lips on mine, his heavy breaths mixing between every passionate kiss. His tongue trails the cut on my lip as he clutches both sides of my face in his palms, running his fingers up and into my damp hair.

His cock hardens and he rocks himself into my hand, his climax following in an explosive burst.

I stroke him until I'm sure he's finished and nudge our bodies toward the slowed stream of water.

A perma-grin cakes itself on Dash's handsome face. "That was hot." He presses his lips gently to my forehead and reaches for the lever to pull down the remains of our water supply. It might not be much, but it'll be enough to wash the sex off us.

My gaze lingers to his back, my jaw clenching at the sight of scars that litter his beautiful skin. I extend my hand but don't touch him. It seems a more personal thing than something you discuss with a random hookup.

"They were there from *before*." Dash catches the

shift in my attention and chooses to answer me anyway. "I had no idea until Bo blurted it out one day when I was changing."

"You don't remember how they happened?"

Dash pulls me into the water, lathering the soap and gently cleaning my stomach. "Nope. And I'm kind of glad I don't."

I glance up at him. "You know we can't tell them about this, right?"

His smile fades and he nods. "Yeah."

I graze his cheek with my knuckles. "It can be our little secret."

"Will you promise me something?" Dash tucks my hair behind my ear.

"Maybe, what is it?"

"When the time comes for you to betray us, will you at least warn me?" He sighs and lowers his voice. "I won't try to stop you; I just want to know if it'll be the last time I see you."

"I..."

The door to the shower creaks open and a throat clears. "How cute." Bo leans against the wooden wall and looks me up and down. "When's my turn?"

"In your fucking dreams." I don't bother concealing my body. He's already gotten a peek, might as well give him something to ingrain into his memory since that's all he'll ever have of my body.

Bo shrugs. "In due time, Birdie. I have no doubt you'll be begging for it in the future."

Dash grabs his shirt and covers my front with it. "Seriously, Bo? Do you have to be so vulgar?"

"I'm the vulgar one? You're fucking the enemy." He snorts. "Wait until Wes finds out. His mutt will tear you apart."

Keeping me alive is one thing, but why would Wes care if I had sex with Dash? That doesn't screw with his plan at all. If anything, it benefits him.

Dash steps into his pants and I drag my clothes off the side of the shower. They're still moist but I didn't exactly expect them to be dry by the time I was finished. I toss Dash his shirt and slide my garments onto my body anyway. As much as I'm enjoying teasing Bo with something he'll never have, I'd rather feel the thick armor weighing my body down than be without it. A sort of protective blanket I've grown fond of over the years, saving me from death more times than I can count.

"Tell him then, I dare you." I buckle the top of my shirt in place. "Go ahead. We'll wait here. If he's going to react the way you're implying, he'll end your life first just for being the messenger." I slide my feet into my boots. "Or are you afraid of him? Is that it? Because he's clearly more powerful than you, that much is obvious."

"You bitch." Bo grits his teeth and then snarls, exposing his fangs at me. "I should have sucked the life out of you when I had the chance."

I approach him, pausing to pat his shoulder as I pass. "You're right, you should have." I walk away, leaving him behind to stew at my truthful accusations. He's well aware that Wes is the dominant one in their little trio, and for some unknown reason, he's overly protective of me. It wasn't until Bo confirmed that a moment ago that I realized that fully.

Now I just have to figure out how to use that to my advantage.

7

WES

Wren storms into our cabin like she owns the place and goes straight past me and into the bedroom. Dash follows close behind and disappears into the room with her.

Their scent intermingles together, creating an aroma that turns my stomach and stirs my beast.

Calm down, I tell him. *They walked by in tandem, that's all that was.*

A small part of me knows better but refuses to acknowledge the overpowering thought.

Bo slams the door shut, stealing my attention from my spiraling mindset.

"What's wrong with you?" I ask him,

He stalks to the kitchen and rips off a chunk of bread. "Nothing."

Bo is typically pissed about something, so his behavior isn't entirely surprising. But paired with how

Dash and Wren entered, it has my suspicions growing. Did he do something to her? Is he the reason Dash and Wren ignored me and went directly into the room? Bo has attempted on numerous occasions to attack her, did he do so again?

"If you touched her..." My hand hardens into a fist at my side, the heat already bubbling to the surface.

"Me?" Bo laughs. "You think *I* would fornicate with that disgrace? Even I have standards, Wes." He obnoxiously chews the bread, swallowing it down with a gulp of water from the cup near him.

"I thought you did pretty well." Wren's voice echoes through the small space to meet my ears.

I tilt my head, cracking my neck and exhaling. Turning on my heel, I stomp the few feet across our tiny home and barge into the room Dash and Wren are occupying. "Out," I spit at him.

Dash stops fumbling with the vials in his hands and wide eye stares at me.

I partially expected to walk in here and find them *together*, but I was wrong. They're in their typical positions. Dash at the table and Wren sitting on the bed. Am I being overly paranoid for no reason? My beast and his claim of her getting the best of both of us?

"What the fuck?" Wren rises to her feet immediately. "What's your problem?"

"You." I whip my head toward her and furiously point at the bed. "Sit."

She complies, not because she wants to, but

because my beast commanded it. A power he has over only one type of being—one I don't wish to acknowledge. It can't be true. She can't be. I won't allow it.

You have no control over such things, my beast reminds me.

"Wes," Dash mutters. "Don't you—"

"No." I cut him off. "We leave in the morning. Go pack the rest of our supplies."

Dash runs his hand through his hair, and that's when I notice it's damp. Similar to that of Wren's. I suck in a breath, hoping like hell I can maintain the reigns over the beast threatening to rip him apart. I care for Dash. Like a friend. Like a brother. I do not wish him dead. It would go against everything I believe in. I do not kill the innocent.

He is not innocent, the voice demands.

"Now!" A growl escapes me and fire ripples up my chest and out my mouth.

Dash flits his gaze at Wren one last time before exiting the room and leaving the two of us alone.

"What's gotten into you?" She repositions herself on the mattress.

I could ask her the same question, but I won't. I cannot afford to hear the truth, not when my beast is so hellbent on taking what belongs to him. What should not be his that he insists on claiming. What a hopeless fool we both are.

I step into the doorway and lean my back against it. Crossing my arms over my chest, I stare forward and away. I cannot stand to look at her right now—not if I don't want to fall completely apart. There is too much on the line for such things to happen.

When I spared her life, I never expected any of this to happen. I knew in my soul that I couldn't allow her to die but I didn't realize the magnitude of what would follow. I'm still not even sure if I do.

"What, so you're not going to talk to me?" She's annoyed and I can't say that I blame her.

I've been acting like an irrational fool from the second I laid my eyes on her. I never should have allowed any of this to happen, but my beast refused to let me walk away from her. I am supposed to be brutal, fearless, in complete and utter control. But here I am losing my goddamn mind over a female I know nothing about other than the fact that she wants to end my life and eradicate all demons from this realm. Why would my beast decide that she was worthy of his admiration?

You know why.

"You're going to stand there all night? Brooding in silence?" Wren continues to pry, to try to get me to say anything.

But there is nothing that can be said to make sense of any of this. Not to her. Not to me.

I must focus on the task at hand. Getting through the night and the next few days as we embark on this seemingly impossible journey to rescue our people from Rock Bridge. I will leverage her to my advantage and then, when we are finished, I will sever our ties and get as far away from her as possible. Once I have done that, I will continue searching for a way out of this dreaded realm. Then, I will be worlds apart and can end this profane connection.

You will do no such thing.

Wait and see.

"Fine." Wren huffs and pats the thin pillow on the bed.

I steal a glance at her out of the corner of my eye, and watch as she attempts to get comfortable on the rather stiff and rough mattress. I stay firmly in place at my post, fully prepared to stand here all night if I have to. I will not permit Dash or Bo to enter this room without my consent.

I spend my time studying the wood frame of the doorway across from me. I count the splinters blistering off the poorly built structure to distract myself from the irregular breathing of the woman only a few feet away. No matter what I consume myself with I cannot detach my thoughts from her. There's this visceral desire to know her, to enter her mind and discover every inch of her soul that she has never shared with another. My beast argues that he already has this knowledge but that would be impossible, completely improbable, given we only just encountered her a few days ago. He insists he's known her his whole existence. One soul that was split in two and dropped into beings that would eventually reunite one day. If that's the case, the universe really has it out for me by making my mate a fucking hunter. More specifically the one with the highest acclaimed title. And if my beast were correct in his ramblings, wouldn't Wren know those too? He must be mistaken and the sooner I get him to realize that, the better.

Still, it doesn't stop the intense urge I have to gravitate toward her. To protect her. To shield her from any harm that comes her way and defend her honor. If only there were a way to shut this off. To no longer feel these feelings and think these thoughts. It serves me no purpose since she will never be mine.

Seconds turn into minutes. The time ticking by at both an impossibly quick and painfully slow pace. Part of me wants to pause it, to stand here in her presence until the end of days. I would accept the small gift of this nearness even if it meant nothing more. But with that thought, I realize I cannot keep her forever, and the sooner day breaks, the closer the realness of detaching myself from this horribly toxic situation.

Both Bo and Dash quit stirring and eventually claim the available sleep spaces as their own, drifting off into the last comfortable slumber I assume they will have for a while. There's no telling what the coming days will bring. We have a plan, but it's shotty at best.

Wren whimpers. The softness of her cry pivoting my body toward her. I squint, scanning her petite shape through the darkness and searching for any sign of harm.

She's on her side, facing the wall, her back toward

the room. Her knees pulled to her chest and her body trembling.

An ache rumbles in my core at the very sight of her distress.

Her hand clenches the bedding and her body twitches.

My feet betray me, taking silent steps toward her. I kneel next to her and hold my breath as I watch the goosebumps on her flesh prickle. Carefully, I rest the back of my hand against her bare skin. She's ice-cold to the touch.

I latch onto the measly blanket at the foot of the bed and drape it over her body in hopes that she will warm soon, and the quivering of her body will stop. I rest against the wall next to the bed and wait for it to take effect. Those seconds turn into minutes. All of which does nothing to rid her of her discomfort. I grow tired of watching her struggle, her body still reeling from the injuries and no doubt the shock of her current situation. Going to bed with damp hair did her no favors, either.

Get in with her, my beast commands.

Instead of following through with his order, I sit back along the edge and reach my hand toward her. I allow my power to come to the surface, warming my skin without catching it ablaze. I place it under the blanket and hope that it will be enough to help regulate her temperature.

She stirs and for a second, I'm afraid she will wake

and catch me this close to her. That she will ask me questions that I shouldn't answer. I do not want to lie to her... I cannot lie to her. Telling her the truth would only complicate things much worse than they already are.

Wren flips over to face me, and I freeze. She throws her arm over mine, the coolness of her skin desperate for the warmth of mine. I don't dare move, not yet, not while she's teetering on the brink of consciousness.

She nestles her head against the pillow and tugs my arm toward her, clutching it to her chest. Her damp armor hints as to why she cannot get warm. Between her wet hair and clothes, to the pathetic accommodations I've given her, she's had no fighting chance.

I increase my heat level without harming her and will her shakes to dissolve. Ignoring my beast's desire to climb in and press my body to hers, I do what I can to make her comfortable while maintaining somewhat of a distance. Although, my skin pressed to her bare chest is not much space at all. My beast and I revel in the temporary pleasure it brings us.

I study her breathing, noting each irregularity and quiver that leaves her. Minute's pass and it evens out, her body relaxing to the warmth that mine provides. She clings to me, reminding me just how dainty she is compared to my stature. It's a strange reality that this small being is as powerful and feared as she is in our world.

She doesn't let go of my arm and I don't pry it away.

Perhaps I'm being selfish in wanting to hold onto this moment a bit longer. The calm before the storm I can only imagine will come raging down on us in the coming days.

I lay my head to the side, relaxing as I bring her the smallest amount of peace. I get lost in the steady rise and fall of her chest and ignore the intrusive thoughts that follow. I don't want to imagine her and Dash being together—it's a vision I cannot stomach. I refuse the truth of it no matter how real it may be. His scent still mixed with hers in a way that could only be from...

Kill him, my beast growls.

You'll wake her, stop.

The selfish bastard shuts up, knowing that if we disturb her, this might end all too soon.

8

WREN

I wake to find Wes slung over the side of the bed, his warm hand resting on my forearm. I pull myself away from him while watching his motionless face. From this close, I can examine every freckle and scar littering his skin—the long, wispy lashes that line his eyes, and the plushness of his lips.

It should feel wrong to have him this near, but instead, it's strangely comforting.

Enemy, I remind myself.

What could have possibly provoked him to choose such a sleep position anyway? Because he refused to let me out of his sight? So he would be sure he'd wake if I stirred and wanted to sneak out? Regardless of the reasoning, it appears absurdly uncomfortable. His neck twisted to the side; his large frame contorted as he clings to stay upright.

Has he been that way long?

A small part of me wants to stay here and watch him sleep. There's something oddly mesmerizing about being this close to someone so off-limits. I've snuck up on demons in the past. I've slit their throats while they slumbered, but I never stopped to admire one as they slept, caught up in their peculiar beauty. That type of thing is forbidden. Taboo. Against our basic hunter nature.

I poke Wes gently on the cheek.

His eyes flicker open, slow at first, but then, as if realizing that he shouldn't be here, he jumps to his feet, wiping at his chin.

"Were you drooling?" I ask him with a smile.

He shakes his head. "No, of course not. My apologies, I must have dozed off."

"Mmhm. And was there a reason as to why you insisted on sleeping on the side of my bed?" I hop off the edge, in the space between him and my mattress, and adjust the buckles on my top, making sure they're snug in place.

"You were..." He pauses momentarily. "Cold."

I stop what I'm doing and hesitate before fully looking up at him. "Cold?" I narrow my gaze at him.

"Yes." He holds his hand up and his skin begins glowing. "Built-in heater."

I recall my slumber, trying desperately to go to sleep when I was annoyed at Wes for posting up at my door. It's one thing when he does it outside the room, but he made it a point to make it known he was keeping guard. And the way he treated Dash was unacceptable. Between my aggravation with him, and the wet clothes I wore to bed, it was rather difficult to get comfortable enough to rest. It took me what felt like forever until I dozed off, only to have night terrors and a chill I couldn't seem to shake.

I briefly dreamt of a fire, warm and inviting. I was wrapped in a thick, heavy blanket that cloaked me from the frost nipping at my body. I clung to it and refused to let go, for once feeling like I had found a safe place to rest my head.

And this whole time, that was *Wes* that brought on that comfort? What the actual fuck?

"Oh," is all I can manage to say.

Wes clears his throat and rubs at his neck. "I…" He points to the open door. "Should get my things ready so we can head out."

I nod. "Yeah, obviously." I'd do the same, but it's not exactly like I have any of my own stuff here. I'll have to rely on whatever they bring to serve us on this journey. One that will no doubt end in all of us dead. There's no way in hell they could ever get what they want and get away with it. Not when the number of hunters far outweigh the demons. But, despite the odds being against us, I have to try, otherwise I'll never get them to tell me how to cure this beacon on my neck. And right now, that's all I care about.

Wes awkwardly goes to leave the room when Dash approaches.

"I need to get supplies." He motions toward the table full of his herbs and salves.

Wes sighs. "Be quick."

"Sure thing." Dash steps around him and into the room. "Hey," he shyly says as he comes closer.

"Is there anything I can do to help?" I approach and stand there a bit out of place, unsure of what the heck I'm supposed to be doing.

Dash scans the contents of the disorganized table. "Do you see the mugwort anywhere?"

I grab the vial of familiar-looking leaves and extend it toward him. "Here."

Dash smiles and takes it from me, securing it into the satchel at his side. "What about Satan's breath?"

"I'm afraid I don't know what that one looks like." Still, I look through and try to locate it.

"Ah. Here it is." He plucks one with a dark reddish powder inside and places it with the others, the bottles gently clanging against one another. Dash snatches a few more and then scratches at his chin. "What am I forgetting?"

"What about that feverfew?" I nod to a small bottle with tiny white flowers that have a round, yellow center.

"Good call." He takes it without a second thought and lets out a breath. "That should do."

I skim the remains in search of the healing tonic he had given me prior, only to find that it's missing. He must have already placed it into his bag, meaning that maybe I can commandeer it from him later and down the rest of it in hopes I can recuperate quicker. I'll need all the strength I can muster if I'm going to get through the next few days. I'm not sure how effective the tonic is considering nothing about my stay here has been normal. I shouldn't even be standing as it is, given the injuries I sustained. Between whatever magic Wes did on my leg, and that of the tonic, I've bounced back far better than I could have imagined in the short amount of time. Why stop here though? I'd rather be at full capacity in the company of these men, especially when it's likely they'll turn on me at any moment.

"You jealous?" I overhear Bo say from the main area of their small house.

A mild growl fills the space next, and when I step out of the bedroom, I smile at Bo's hands raised in the air in front of him.

Any chance of that sick bastard being put in his place is a win in my book.

Bo latches his sights onto me and winks. "And there she is."

I ignore the way Wes's entire body seems to stiffen at my arrival. He turns slowly, glancing over his shoulder. "Here." He holds a satchel in my direction. "Your supplies."

Continuing to disregard their obnoxious masculinity, I march over and pluck the thing from his hand, pulling it open and rummaging through the meager contents. "Is this a joke?"

I blink up at him.

Bo slides a long dagger off the counter and secures it in the sheath on his waistband.

"You trust *him* with a weapon but all I get is *this*?" A few rations and something that could be used as either a blanket or a pillow. I guess I'll have to decide which is more important when the time comes.

Wes stands there firmly in place. "I barely trust you with that."

He twitches slightly, almost like he doesn't believe his words fully. But if that's the case, why am I only equipped with the very barest of essentials?

Bo chuckles. "What, Birdie, you don't think we can protect you?" He wraps his arm around Wes's shoulder.

Wes immediately shrugs him off. "Don't touch me."

"I don't need anyone to protect me," I say through gritted teeth.

"Mmhm, well, if I'm not mistaken, you're alive because of us." Bo steps toward me. He brings his index finger to my chin, tapping it gently. "I'd be grateful if I were you." His warm breath lingers against my cheek.

I glare up at him. "I'd kill myself if I were *you*."

Bo grins. "Those are fighting words."

I steady my mind and assess numerous scenarios. I could grab the knife from his waistband and shove it between a soft spot in his ribs in hopes of penetrating something vital enough to kill him. I could slit his throat with it, but considering how tall he is, he could snatch it from me in time, and then use it on me. If I manage to pull off the first option, I'd have to act swiftly and end Wes's life, too. But from this position and his control over me, I'm not sure if I could gain the upper hand. And then, well, there's Dash I'd have to deal with. Could I bring myself to harm someone so... Dash? It's not his fault he got wrapped up in the wrong crowd. It could have easily been hunters who found and influenced him to join their cause instead.

As far as I know, the only thing Dash has done wrong is keep terrible company.

Does that mean he deserves to die?

"Can you two give it a rest?" Wes shoves his arm between me and Bo and nudges us apart, ending any chance I had at seizing that microscopic opportunity.

The odds weren't exactly in my favor anyway. Given I'm spending the next few days with these idiots, there has to be another that has a higher probability of success.

Not to mention, Bo holds the key to ridding my neck of his mark, so maybe I shouldn't be so hasty in ending his life just yet. Couldn't it have been Wes that marked me instead, leaving me the freedom to purge this realm of the demonic scum that is Bo?

"You know...I'm really enjoying this." Bo goes back to the counter to retrieve the rest of his belongings.

"Yeah, that much I'm aware, dumbass." Wes throws his bag over his shoulder and settles his sights on me. "You're not getting a weapon; not right now. You won't need it."

"Marching me into enemy territory unarmed makes all the sense. Why don't you just kill me and get it over with?" I've gone into battle with less before, but that didn't mean I wouldn't, at the very least, *try* not to be so vulnerable.

Dash appears from the tiny living room, his own bag secured to his body. "They've kept me alive, even when I had no idea how to fight. Put a little faith in them for the time being."

Wes steps toward the door, gripping the handle and tugging it open. "With Bo's venom flowing through your veins, you'll smell like him, not like you. They won't see you as the enemy."

An easy way for me to pick a few of them off and gain a little strength.

"Don't draw attention to yourself," Wes continues. "Most demons are too narrow-minded and egotistical to notice anyone other than their own reflection."

He's not wrong there. Demons are arrogant as can be.

Bo reeks of textbook demonic behavior. Wes on the other hand...he's unlike anything I've ever come across. Confident, but not quite cocky. And not only did he save me, but he took Dash in, too. Hell, even Bo gets a brownie point for helping Dash stay alive despite it not benefiting him in some way.

I step through the threshold of their cabin and out onto the creaky porch. The brisk morning air nips my cheeks and soaks its way into my lungs with each breath. Structures often bring safety, but nature, nature provides freedom. Just this little bit gives me hope that maybe I'll make it out of this nightmare after all.

Bo shoves past me, nudging my shoulder and reminding me of his revolting existence.

"Excuse you." I dust off the spot he touched me and straighten my armor.

Dash comes around my side and offers me a weak smile, then glances up at Wes, who takes his place in front of us.

Wes clears his throat. "Our first stop is Breckenridge. We should arrive by dusk if we don't encounter any trouble. Stay alert, stay close, and do not try to run." His gaze bores into me with his last few words.

Their meaning seeping its way into my chest and rooting itself within me.

My lips part and the intent of asking him what the fuck kind of power he has over me is right on the tip of my tongue. But I keep the thought to myself, because if I'm right, Bo and Dash have no idea that he can do this. And if Bo finds out, there's no telling what he'll expect Wes to do with that authority. Instead, I'll bide my time until I can question Wes without Bo's prying ears and eyes.

What's bizarre is that Wes could have already abused this ability, but he hasn't. He's only used it on a few rare occasions. What could he possibly gain from sparingly compelling me? Does he think I don't know he can do this? That I can't feel his words root their way into my core and lock onto my free will? Maybe he's trying not to be obvious so he can use the skill more effectively at another time? Clearly, *he's* aware he's doing it, right? Does it consume an excess of his energy? Or use some kind of power of his that he doesn't want to dwindle? There must be a reason why he's not mistreating this influence over me. It might just take me a bit longer to figure it out.

"I won't," I finally mutter to assure these three that I will follow along for the time being. It serves me no purpose in running now, not when I'm still weak, have no idea where I am, and have a glaring alpha marker on my neck. Not *glaring* glaring. It's barely noticeable if you don't go looking for it. My hair pretty much covers it up to the unknowing eye. But the second Bo and I get close to that boundary point, the thing will go off like a beacon for any demon in the close vicinity, alerting them to a tasty meal.

I'd prefer not to be eaten by anyone, let alone a repulsive monster. And most definitely not one that is keen to the information of a warrior soul's yielding power if consumed. I don't want to be the reason the realms are reopened and more of their kind contaminate our home. Prania is still recovering from the war of the realms and can't afford the damage another war would no doubt cause.

"Scout ahead." Wes nods toward an area that looks vaguely the same as each direction I turn.

It must be some kind of illusion spell, which is no

doubt what protects them from hunters finding their cabin.

I'll add casting abilities to the list of things they can do. That, or they're in cahoots with a witch or warlock. I wouldn't be surprised. At this point, if Wes and Bo sprouted wings and flew away, it wouldn't be that alarming. Most of the witches went underground though, quite literally. With their blood lingering on both the light and dark scale depending on the magic they cast, it puts them somewhere in the middle between both sides. Most hunters see them as traitors though and will kill on sight without even hearing them out. The little bit of darkness is one less demonic being in our realm. I've taken out my fair share, but they were on the far end of the spectrum, worshiping at least one of the Princes of Hell.

Their beliefs didn't matter to me though. I kill who I'm tasked to kill. I don't ask questions. I do my job and up until a few days ago, I was damn good at it.

That's not to say there have never been issues. I've had my hands full with beastly opponents in the past, but there hasn't been a single target I haven't been capable of eliminating. I've spent weeks pursuing jobs, days in battle, and fought fierce demons. Sometimes one after another. And these two here, their fate has been sealed. They will join their place with the others once I find an opportunity to redeem myself of this failed mission.

9

DASH

I'm fairly certain Wes hates me.

Bo has never really liked me, and I don't think that will ever change. I'm okay with that. He tolerates me. He helps keep me alive. For what reason, I'm not entirely sure, but I accept his assistance and occasional disregard either way.

Wes, on the other hand, has always been kind to me. Warm. Inviting. Never cold and shut off like Bo.

Bo acts like he doesn't have a heart, and I wouldn't be all that surprised if it were a true statement. That perhaps he has something else fueling his lifeforce. Stale bread and ale are the only two things he seems to get excited about. Well, that, and killing. Hunters, demons, witches, fae, vampires, werewolves—you name it, Bo will slaughter it. He doesn't really discriminate. Basically, if it looks at him wrong, it's fair game.

Luckily for me, I've managed to not piss Bo off

enough for him to end my life. And up until recently, I thought Wes would be the person to reinforce that belief that I wasn't on the menu for dinner.

Now, Wes can barely meet my gaze, and the few times he does, he suppresses a snarl that rises from his chest. His beast is mad. No, his beast is furious. But why? Because I slept with Wren? She's a hunter, why would any of them care? If anything, they should be grateful that she doesn't hate at least one of us. I'm not convinced she won't butcher us the first chance she gets, but if she does, maybe the little bit of a relationship I've formed with her will aid in my ability to reason with her. It's wishful thinking, that much I'm aware of.

I've spent enough time with Bo to know that those carnal desires are often impossible to turn off. And despite Bo and Wren hating each other, they're more alike than they think.

They are both passionate about their beliefs. And they are determined to kill anyone that crosses them. Unfortunately for them, they're at far ends of the spectrum, naturally wanting nothing more than to rip each other's throats out.

Wes is brutal, too, but he's rational. He doesn't kill just to kill the way Bo and Wren do. He does it to survive. He's able to separate his distaste for Wren's kind enough to not go seeking them out. He actually tries to avoid hunters at all costs unless necessary. And if it weren't for the distress call that we overheard that day, he wouldn't have rushed to that dodgy side of town and did what he could to save a few demons who got caught in the crossfire.

I wasn't there to witness the fight firsthand, but I could barely believe my own eyes when I saw him pick her nearly lifeless body off the ground and bring her back to the cabin. I should have realized then that she was something to him, but in all my time with these two guys, I never would have imagined that kind of connection happening with a hunter.

It goes against their fundamental nature.

I may not have a vast knowledge of this world with my limited memory, but I know enough to know that kind of thing is off-limits—let alone highly unlikely.

I didn't mean to overstep by having sex with her. And a large part of me doesn't regret it at all. I have no recollection of being with a woman in any capacity and given how dangerous this life is, I didn't realize I was missing it until I saw her. From that very first moment, I was drawn to her. Something about how in this dark and gloomy existence, there was this brightness she exuded, regardless of her title. She might be Furla Ain, but she's still Wren.

A strong but damaged, delicate flower.

Maybe it was from seeing something so deadly be so incredibly vulnerable. It was like that veil was lifted and I could finally view her not as a hunter but as a woman.

I've never had those immediate desires to kill the

way Wes and Bo do. The way everyone else in this dreaded realm does. I've never really fit in. That much has always been obvious. But I still hung onto the hope that maybe not everybody wanted to kill each other. Or at the very least there could be some good in the seemingly endless darkness.

Somehow, I knew deep down that she wasn't all bad. I clung to that, and put faith in the fact that if I showed her a little kindness, she might reciprocate. That she was probably just doing the same thing Wes and Bo were doing—surviving. She was fighting for what she believed in and what she was taught. I don't blame her for being the way she is and if anything, I applaud how she embraces it with such a truly admirable tenacity. She became the greatest of her kind. Similar to that of Wes and Bo.

Which leads me back to the topic at hand—how was I supposed to know Wes's beast felt the way he did when it's completely unheard of?

It's not exactly like he informed us. Maybe Bo would back off if he knew what she meant to Wes. Maybe I wouldn't have had sex with her if he simply communicated a bit better.

I sigh, because that would mean I wouldn't have experienced her tight and wet...

Bo slaps my arm and drags my attention from the growing erection in my pants. "We're going to take a break over here."

"Right. Yeah." I nod and blink to try to erase the

image of her petite body from my mind. Following the three of them to the fallen logs, I pull the bag off my shoulder and claim a free spot.

"Do I even want to ask what you were lost in thought about?" Bo slides in next to me.

I swallow, briefly glancing over at the oblivious Wren and Wes across from us. "No. Probably not."

"I could guess." Bo breaks off a chunk of cheese and passes the larger hunk to me.

"I'd rather you didn't." I repeat his motion and give the rest to Wes, who breaks off his share and offers Wren the remains.

She takes it without saying anything and bites off a corner, chewing the mouthful slowly and scanning the forest behind me. Wren swallows and glances over her shoulder. "Any idea how far out we are?"

"Another two hours or so." Wes extends his canteen toward her and waits while she takes a long swig and returns it to him. He drinks some and then puts the thing back into his bag. "We've made decent time." He tilts his head toward the sky but when he lowers it, his eyes glow red, his beast rising to the surface.

"What is it?" I ask him, knowing damn well trouble is no doubt about to follow.

Wes brings his index finger gently to his lips and gazes at each one of us.

Bo whispers. "How many?" His ears perk at trying to figure out the answer himself.

"At least four," Wren answers. She closes her eyes

for a moment and draws in a breath before opening, only now, a sly grin is on her beautiful face. "Make that six; more incoming."

Wes nods and Bo tips his head in some unspoken agreement.

Wren scans the ground and slowly latches onto a stick that's near her. She grips it in her hand and sets the rest of her cheese off to the side.

In the blink of an eye, shadows appear from every direction, various shapes and sizes, all hurtling toward us.

"Get behind me," Bo yells at me.

Wes repeats the same words to Wren, attempting to shove her body out of the line of fire.

"Fat fucking chance." She darts around him and shoves the blunt end of the stick right into the neck of an oncoming demon.

Wes exhales a puff of literal smoke. "You're going to get yourself killed." His beast growls and rises to the surface, his body glowing and flames nipping at the surface of every inch of him. He turns on his heel and snatches a dagger mid-air as it's flying toward his head and tosses it to Wren. "Don't make me regret this." He rushes over and snaps the neck of the mangy half-wolf-looking thing that threw the weapon at him.

I keep my back to Bo, my gaze wide and flickering in each direction. Bodies drop all around me despite my lack of participation in the battle.

"Uhh, little help here," Bo groans from behind me.

Four demons ascend on him, two of them launching themselves into the air.

Bo jumps out of the way in time and the monsters land on all fours, their bodies morphing into a vicious canine of sorts. Bo extends his arm and slices at the closest one with his razor-sharp talons. The beast yelps and black blood oozes out of the wound. The thing falls over on its side whimpering in pain.

One of the remaining three latches its sights on me and advances. I steady myself and step backward, hoping that I can draw the attention away from Bo long enough he can finish the other two off. This one remains unshifted, yet no less terrifying.

"Come and get me, you disgusting mutt," I yell at it.

Mid being attacked, Bo lets out a chuckle. "Good one."

Gripping the handle of the knife in my grasp, I wait for the opportunity to strike. I may not have supernatural abilities like my companions, but I do have one advantage—I'm often underestimated. Sure, it might not seem like much, but it almost always results in my attackers letting their guard down and exposing some kind of weakness.

I stop when my heel brushes up against something sturdy. I glance at the tree behind me and steady myself on it as I wait for the monster to continue to advance on me. I note its languid steps and cocky grin. The mostly man, part beast, licks at its exposed fangs and scratches just under one of the horns protruding out of his forehead. It's like he's going on a leisurely afternoon stroll through the woods and that's exactly how I want him to act. I want him to think this is going to be easy.

Shifting my vision past him, I spot Wren on top of a demon, thrusting her dagger in and out of his chest, and Wes blasting waves of flames at a group that comes toward him. Bo struggles with the beast-man and beast creature that are still on him, but it isn't nothing he can't handle. I've seen him battle an entire swarm of hybrid vampires and come out on top.

The thing approaching me smirks. "You think your friends are coming to save you? That's cute."

No, but that's what I want him to assume.

I swallow, painting on my best acting face. It doesn't take much. Regardless of my sly puppy dog act, I really am shaking on the inside. "Oh, it speaks."

"I'm going to enjoy this..." The beast steps directly in front of me and throws his fist up on the tree beside my head. He breathes in deeply and inhales my scent.

The split second he closes his eyes to savor the aroma, I slide my partially hidden knife out and use all my might to shove it directly into the spot just under his armpit.

His dark orange eyes widen and blood trickles from his mouth. He stumbles, and I yank out the serrated blade and move out of his path as he clutches the tree.

Satisfaction rolls over me at having duped such a fierce creature. I am merely a pathetic human in this realm, and I have somehow managed to stay alive this long. Granted, I owe many thanks to Bo and Wes, but they taught me well.

With a smile on my face, I turn toward the action, the feeling is immediately drained out of me as I see a terrible sight unfold.

Dagger clutched in her grasp and ready to be thrown in the direction of Bo and the man he's still wrestling with. The two guys tumble and kick up dust, snapping their jaws while they hold each other back. Demon blood pools on the ground around them and I'm not sure who it's coming from. Although, if Bo is having this much trouble, I can only imagine he's injured in some capacity.

My eyes go wide, and I dig in my heels and take off in a sprint toward the two. Life seems to get stuck in slow motion as I frantically try to get there in time and stop what's about to happen. But it's no use, I'll never make it there before her dagger does.

I watch as it soars through the air, my heart aching in my chest and wishing like hell I had supernatural speed to rush over and snatch it mid-air. I scream but it doesn't matter. Wes is fighting his own battle and could never make it in time either.

Wren is using Wes's distraction and the perfect opportunity to eliminate Bo. I can't say I blame her, given how poorly he's treated her, but not only is he the only thing that can cure her alpha bite, he's not so bad once you get to know him. I'd even go so far to say he's a decent guy. A bit murderous, obviously.

The blade makes a dull thud upon impact and the guys both stop moving and fall on top of one another. Between the dust floating through the thick air and the tears welling up in my eyes, I can't make out a damn thing until I skid to a halt beside them.

A loud groan fills the space and I firmly grip the knife in my own hand, ready to end another demon's life to end this nonsense.

One of the bloodied bodies is shoved to the side and the other struggles to sit up.

My breath hitches when I realize it's Bo emerging from the chaos, dirt and demon gore caked on his entire body.

"Fuck, man." He laughs and slides the dagger Wren had thrown out of the beast and rises to his feet. Bo tosses the thing to Wren as she approaches. "About damn time."

Wren catches it with ease and smiles. "You wouldn't stop flopping around long enough for me to get a clear shot."

Wes jogs over to join us, a look of surprise no doubt matching the one on my face.

Bo raises his hand toward her. "High five," he says when she doesn't seem to understand.

She slaps his palm and then points at his leg. "You're injured." A slight hint of concern lines her features.

She and Bo both turn toward me.

Bo speaks first, "What's with the look?"

I blink at him and then at her.

"Are you okay?" She asks while her gaze scans my body.

Wes interjects. "The dagger, Wren." He holds out his hand and clenches his jaw.

"What?" She tilts her head in his direction.

"The dagger, I won't repeat myself." Wes lets out a low grumble.

"Are you fucking serious?" She points to Bo. "I just saved his ass."

She did. Which is somehow more surprising than when I thought she was going to kill him the first chance she got. I wanted to hope and believe there was good in her, so why am I shocked the moment that becomes a reality? Wes seems to be thinking the same thing. Or at least, some version of it. He doesn't trust her, that much is certain. Wasn't this all his idea after all?

"I have to agree with Birdie on this one." Bo steadies himself on his good leg.

"This isn't up for debate." Wes continues to hover his hand there in place. "Give it to me, or I will take it from you. The choice is yours."

As much as I think it would make for an interesting fight, I don't want to see either one of them hurt, especially inflicted by each other.

"Whatever." Wren surprises me once more and gives Wes the dagger. She's feisty enough that I thought for sure she would have chosen the more complicated route.

"Seriously? Giving up so easily, Birdie?" Bo stumbles and falls to the ground. "Whoa."

The three of us that remain drop down with him.

"I don't feel so hot." Bo's head spins and he blinks repeatedly.

"It's a claw," Wren declares. She tears at his pant leg to expose the wound. "See that, it must have broken off in there and is just continually poisoning you." She nods to the body she had thrown the dagger into. "What is that?"

Wes grips the man-beast's shoulder and flips it onto its back. "Drakka."

"Are you sure?" She cranes her neck to get a better view of the fallen demon.

"Positive," Wes says with a hint of annoyance in his voice.

"Okay." Wren exhales. "Does anyone have a knife that doesn't have demon guts all over it? I need to get this thing out before it continues to burrow its way into his leg."

Bo slips a clean blade from his side and gives it to her. "Will this work?"

She nods and turns toward me. "I need you two to hold him down." She focuses on Bo for a second. "This is going to hurt."

Bo grins. "Give me your worst."

Wes latches onto Bo's thigh and I grip Bo's ankle, both of us holding him in place like she asked.

"Once I get this thing out, I'll need your flame, Wes." She eyes him briefly and goes to work, wasting no more time by digging the sharp end of the blade into the swollen flesh.

Dark blood seeps out and Bo flinches only the smallest amount.

I glance up at his stoic face. He's a better man than me for tolerating this so well.

Wren continues digging the knife into his leg for another second before shoving her thumb and index finger into the opening and rooting around.

"Oh yeah, that's the spot," Bo grumbles.

"Why do I get the feeling you're weirdly enjoying this?" Wren counters with her fingers digging around his wound. "Got it." She seems to latch onto something and yanks it out through the slit and holds it in front of her for a moment, then tosses it to the side. Picking up the knife, she looks to Wes. "Flame, please."

He complies, snatching the blade from her and blasting it with a wave of fire.

Wren clutches the glowing thing and presses it against Bo's oozing cut. It sizzles and smoke rolls off his flesh.

"Ah, fuck me," Bo grits his teeth.

"You wish." Wren finishes applying pressure to the wound and stands, wiping the blade on her pant leg.

"Here." She extends its handle first to Wes, who takes it and gives it back to a rising Bo.

"Well, that was fun." Bo shakes some of the dirt off himself and applies a bit of pressure to his injured leg.

"You okay?" I ask him, because what the hell else am I supposed to say in a moment like this.

"Mmhm. My body should heal itself soon now that the toxin is out of my system. I knew something was fucking wrong when I didn't recover immediately. Fucking Drakka are an abomination."

"I could say the same thing about you." Wren winks at him and strolls over to our makeshift campsite. She rummages through the wreckage and points to something. Snatching it off a rock, she grins. "There you are." Wren bites into the remains of her cheese and comes back over. "What?" She looks between us. "No sense in being wasteful."

I shift to peer at all the dead bodies around us and can't help but wonder what my life entailed prior to losing my memory. Was I surrounded by death and destruction? My muscle memory kicked in when I was intimate with Wren, but it never has when I've been in battle. Does that mean my existence before this was free of such things? Or was I fighting to live every day of that time, too? Will I ever know the truth about who I am or where I came from? Why has no one ever come looking for me? Maybe not knowing is better, but that doesn't make the questions stop coming.

10
WREN

We make it to the outskirts of Breckenridge without any other major issues.

There was the mild dispute of Wes not wanting to give me privacy so I could take a leak, and then him being dramatic when Dash offered to stand guard. Bo volunteered, too, to get Wes to shut up, but there's no way I'm letting him anywhere near me with my pants down.

Sure, I saved his life, but he is the only thing that can rid me of this damn alpha marker.

Did the idea of soaring that dagger into his chest cross my mind? Watching in what I can only imagine would have been pure bliss as the blade pierced his heart? Ab-so-fucking-lutely.

But I'm not a complete fucking idiot.

I have to keep reminding myself to be strategic if I want out of this alive.

And the added satisfaction of Bo giving me a split moment of respect when I rescued his ass was definitely a solid trade-off.

Ultimately, I was able to piss by myself, using the leverage that I did, in fact, save the unruly demon, and that if I wanted to escape, I would have when they were all distracted. If I didn't have the mark on my neck, I undeniably would have taken that out when it presented itself. Although, I'm not sure they'd give me the amount of leash that I currently have if I didn't have the constant reminder that I cannot leave permanently on my body.

I'm at their mercy for the time being and we all are aware of that.

And yet, it came as a complete shock to Dash that I spared Bo's life.

I shouldn't be surprised he was concerned for his friend, especially after asking me to let him know when, not if, I would betray them. I guess he knew the time was coming at some point and thought that it was then. I never did promise him one way or the other and it's not exactly like I owe him anything. But somehow it stings a little that he actually thought I would go through with it like that.

"We're not going to just waltz up there are we?" I reach out and stop Wes from going any further.

His serious gaze trails down to my hand on his arm and up to meet mine. For a split second, his demeanor hardens and softens and hardens again, like there's some internal conflict going on that I'm unaware of the details.

"Sure thing, Birdie." Bo slaps me on the back.

The commotion from inside the local establishments floats out toward us in our covered area right on the edge of town. Now, we're hidden by a vast forest, but the second we step through this tree line, we're exposed to anyone within an eyesight distance. We're no doubt already in range of any supernatural who might be intrigued by our presence, regardless of the natural concealment we've journeyed through all day.

"There shouldn't be any issue if you don't bring attention to yourself." Wes runs his hand through his thick hair. "That thing on your neck makes you blend in with the rest of us."

"And that's supposed to put me at ease? You do remember who I am, right? That might not mean much to you three...but I have a reputation."

"What do you expect me to do then, Wren?" Wes sighs heavily. "Would you like me to announce to everyone who you are and say you're under our captivity? Risk every demon in the surrounding area finding out where you are, and maybe inform them of that mark on your neck?"

"I mean, no. I was thinking more along the lines of throwing a shirt or something over this." I point to the thick, black armor hugging my body tightly. "Doesn't it look a little obvious?"

Without meeting their gaze, I'm certain each one of

their eyes goes directly to my cleavage. I don't blame them—it was sort of an open invitation.

"Here." Bo grips the hem of his shirt and tugs it over his head, exposing his chiseled exterior.

I do my best not to study the many lines and curves covering his frame. We are still enemies after all, and I can't afford to see him in any other light.

Bo tosses the dirt and blood-covered thing straight into my face.

I catch it and glare at him. "Really?"

He shrugs. "You asked for it."

"Better?" Wes asks before turning to look through the brush at the small village we've arrived at.

I make the mistake of sniffing the garment as I drag it over my head. "This reeks."

"You want these, too?" Bo latches onto his waistband and unbuttons his pants.

Wes growls at him. "Don't even think about it."

Bo sighs and secures them back in place. "Your loss."

"Don't speak to anyone." Wes looks me straight in the eyes, doing that thing he does so well, tightening that control he has over me.

Fucking bastard.

I open my mouth, but the words don't come. Are you kidding me? His stupid power trip included him, too? What am I supposed to do if there's an issue? Or if I actually *need* to say something? He should really be more specific with his stupid commands.

Whatever.

If that's what he wants, then that's what he'll get.

I break away from them and march my way through the trees, waiting for the idiots to follow. They catch up within a second, Wes and Bo jumping ahead of me and Dash trailing us. I glance over my shoulder and take in the solemn expression on his face.

Demons of many shapes, sizes, and variations loiter about, none of them giving us a second look. Maybe this plan will work after all. A small group of partially shifted werewolves congregate near the entrance to an establishment a few doors down. Dark fae flutter past us, the wind from their wings floating across my cheeks. The scent of so many demonic creatures fills my chest and the need to slaughter every one of them rises to an uncomfortable level.

A wendigo stomps by, flicking up dirt with its every step. The creature's arms are stained red with the blood of its kills. The same substance drips off its chin and the antlers protruding from its skull exposed head. I've never seen one this up close and personal, considering the only time I interact with demons of this caliber is when I'm tasked to eliminate them.

"Kinda creepy, right?" Dash whispers in my ear.

I start to speak, but the words don't come. Instead, I offer him what I think is an acknowledging toothless smile and nod in agreement.

I'm not sure I'd categorize the beast as creepy, as much as I would disgusting and repulsive. But I can't exactly say that, considering Wes had taken my voice from me.

"This way." The asshole points.

I guess I should specify that I'm referring to Wes.

One could easily confuse him and Bo, but with Wes's current behavior, Bo is shining in a much brighter light. I still hate the bastard, but the race for which I dislike more is becoming a closer one by the minute.

I follow Wes up a set of creaky stairs leading to a small tavern. Noise billows out, but not the way it does from all the others we've passed. Hopefully he purposefully chose one with less potential prying eyes.

Wes holds the door open for me and I step inside the quaint establishment, a bit hesitant to go any further into enemy territory. Not a single being glances in our direction.

Bo comes from around me and makes his entrance known. "Tommy," he shouts at the barkeep. He makes his way over and slams his fist on the counter. "Two pitchers of your finest ale and stew for four. Don't forget the bread."

The old man with grey lining not only the thick hair on his head, but his bushy eyebrows and beard, too. "We only have one ale, Bo, you know this." He pauses and perks up one of those brows. "Four?" His lazy gaze trails the direction Bo came from, and stops when he lands on me. "A lady friend?"

I swallow and clench my jaw in hopes of hiding any

bubbling up nerves at being in a place like this. Wes nudges me, and Dash places his hand on the small of my back to guide me over to where Bo is standing.

Bo throws his arm over my shoulder. "She's with me."

"Is that so?" The man grins.

"Birdie, meet Tommy, Tommy, this is Birdie."

"The pleasure is all mine."

I force another pleasant smile and nod, not saying anything because not only do I not want to, but because I can't.

Wes slides a few coins across the wooden surface. "We'll be over there." He points to an empty booth in the corner and leans in. "Know where I can find Frank?"

"Mmhm." Tommy nods. "Evening, Dash, you doing okay?"

Dash reaches over the counter and shakes Tommy's hand. "I'm still kicking, that's about as much as I can ask for. You?"

"Me, too, my boy, me, too."

Bo leads me away from the bar and through the not-so-crowded seating area.

If only I had supernatural hearing so I could listen in on what Wes and Tommy are chatting about where we left them. Who's Frank? And what does he have to do with our plan? Unease rises up within me at not knowing what this other person might entail. I was just starting to figure these three out, and now there's going to be someone else? What if they know who I am and the weight that my soul carries in terms of power?

We pass a table with three mediocre demons. Low-level grunts that I could take out with my eyes closed and my hands tied behind my back. They lack most common knowledge and quite a few brain cells, making them predictable and easy to kill.

One of them flits their gaze up at me as we go by. His muddy brown eyes do a double-take, and he turns to get a better look, drawing unwanted attention my way.

I slide into the booth, my back against the wall, and Bo climbs in next to me, his large frame taking up a considerable amount of space. His leg bumps into mine and I scowl at him.

Dash settles in across from us and cups his head in his hands on the table, his elbows resting on the uneven top.

Something is bothering him, more so than usual. Part of me wants to ask him, to figure out what it is, and see if I can help, but even if I decided to, it's not like I could. Wes has made damn sure of that.

I cast him a glare and watch him disappear around the side of the bar, through a swinging door. I don't enjoy this not knowing thing.

I eavesdrop on the conversation of the men in the bar, doing my best to pick up any useful information I can obtain.

"I wouldn't mess with him," one of the drunken demons slurs.

The other scoffs. "You're afraid of *that*?"

"You haven't heard?"

I peek over at them and watch as the horned demon leans in closer to the other. I strain to listen to his words.

"Rumor has it, he's a..."

The third friend of theirs slams a pitcher of thick, dark liquid onto the table, sloshing it over the edges and disrupting the man from finishing his statement.

Who was he talking about? Bo? Wes? Dash? Clearly, it was one of them. Are these demons familiar with who they are? What they are? Further proof that if they've made such a name for themselves, they are surely the enemy.

I lean against the booth and cross my arms over my chest, waiting for when we can get the hell out of here. This is no place for a hunter. Not when every instinct in my body screams at me to end the life of all the demons in here. Oh, the power I would gain from that, and the less they would have to reopen the gates of the demon realms and unleash more of their kind in Prania.

The pathetic demon who made it a point to crane his neck at me a second ago has repositioned himself in his chair to have a partial view of us. His not-so-obvious attempt to keep an eye on me sets my nerves on edge even more.

Does he recognize me? Does he know who I am? Is

this entire plan about to come unraveled because these fucking idiots thought it was a good idea to bring me to a disgraceful town full of their kind? How did they ever assume no one would recognize my face when I've spent my entire life training for the title I've earned?

I may be overreacting. Despite being Furla Ain, I do pride myself on not allowing my targets to get away, meaning word of me only comes through the whispers of hear-say, not first-hand experience. Unless someone managed to slip away without my knowledge, how would these three half-drunk demons know who I am?

Either way, the incessant dimwit who keeps looking my way needs to stop before I do the thing my hunter instincts are telling me to do—snap this fool's neck.

II
WREN

A short, younger boy drops two pitchers onto our table, the contents overflowing and spilling over the sides. "Sorry," he blurts out and reaches into the apron around his waist to pull out a rag. He makes quick work of cleaning it up, his head lowered the whole time. He scurries away for a moment and returns with four mugs.

"Thanks," Dash tells the kid.

Bo wastes no time filling all but one and giving me and Dash ours. He downs the contents of his own in a solid guzzle, and refills it to the brim. "That's good ale." Bo leans back and throws his arm across the back of our side of the booth.

I eye the cup in front of me, then Dash, who is sipping his. Sighing, I pick the thing up and press it to my lips. I taste the golden liquid, letting the coldness of it melt in my mouth and slide its way down my throat.

It's better than I expect, with its oak and molasses flavor. I gulp down a bit more and wipe the residue off my lips.

"Good, huh?" Bo raises his dark brow at me.

I nod, given that's all I can do.

The boy returns with a plate of bread and cheese, setting it onto our table and walking away like he can't disappear quickly enough.

Bo digs in immediately, ripping off hunks of each and putting some in front of me and Dash, then himself. For such an egotistical demon, he sure is considerate at times. I'll add that to the list of things that don't really make sense.

I scan the crowd for anything out of the ordinary. And by ordinary, I don't mean the countless demons surrounding me. That stupid guy at the table we passed still continues to flit his gaze my way every so often. If I had fangs, I'd expose them and growl at him in an attempt to get him to stop fucking staring.

Bo tilts his head toward me, then follows my line of sight.

The man plays it off like nothing was going on, and carries on talking to his tablemates.

"Is he bothering you?" Bo asks me.

I shake my head and bite into the firm and salty cheese, chewing it with purpose and following it up with a mouthful of bread. I wash it down with the ale and wonder how much longer we'll be in this hell hole.

Wes is nowhere to be found since he vanished

through the door in the far corner in his search for a man named Frank.

I'd ask Bo and Dash what that was all about, but, well, I can't. This whole not being able to talk thing is a real buzzkill.

Speaking of…I swallow the rest of my ale and slide the mug over to Bo.

He refills it without a word and does the same to his own.

"Do you think we could—" Dash begins but stops when the guy with a staring problem scrapes his chair across the floor loudly.

I study the demon's plump form as he stands, and hold my breath in hopes that he doesn't do what I think he's about to.

But the universe is a real bitch, so she sends the guy waltzing in our direction.

I'd mutter the word, *fuck*, if I were allowed.

"What do we have here?" The guy nods toward me.

"None of your business," Bo replies.

"Mmhmm." The guy rubs his bearded chin. "I was thinking…"

Bo stands from his spot, his frame towering over this asshole.

This is where I clarify that it's not Wes. He's still an asshole, as is Bo, but not the asshole I'm referring to at the moment. I should consider calling them asshole one, asshole two, and so on.

"Maybe thinking isn't your strong suit." Bo steps out of the booth and forces the guy to take a step back.

"Come on, man. There's enough to go around."

He better not be referring to me.

"I'll wait my turn." The bastard licks his lips and winks at me.

At this, Dash joins in, rising to his feet and placing his human hands on the man's shoulders. "That's enough."

The man shrugs him off and shoves him. "Don't touch me."

This little bit of interaction causes the other two men this guy was sitting with to stand. The taller of the duo tilts his head, cracking his neck and then his knuckles.

I never understood the point in doing that. Is it supposed to be intimidating? All it shows me is that you're too old and have joint issues.

The shortest of the three, a bald demon with nubbed horns and glowing dark green eyes calls out to his friend. "You good, Storm?"

Storm? What kind of name is that?

Bo steps closer to Storm, again, and comes close to bumping him with his bare chest. He's taunting him, that much is sure. He's giving him the chance to concede, but making his dominance known.

Men and their masculinity.

I stay firmly rooted in the booth, sipping my ale and watching this unfold. I'm pissed, and ready to rip every single one of their throats out, but for the time being, I'm going to let this play out a bit more. Storm will probably cower back to his table and resume being a creep from afar, and Dash and Bo will return to their drinks while we wait for Wes to reappear with, hopefully, some insight to where he went and who this Frank fellow is.

I couldn't be more wrong though. Storm has the audacity to shove Bo, but not before igniting some kind of electrical spark shit that floats off his hands.

Bo growls upon impact and reacts by palming the man's head and slamming it into our table.

Dash's eyes go wide and he ducks to avoid an empty mug flying at his head from across the way, no doubt thrown by one of Storm's buds.

I pour myself some more ale and gulp it down while Bo kicks the shit out of Storm.

He snarls, the beast shifter part of him rising to the surface. Long, sharp claws extend from each fingertip and thick, black scales pop up all over him. A self-made armor I was unaware he possessed. I'll lock that detail away in my mental bank of useful info.

"All over some slut," Storm slurs from his spot on the floor.

I sigh and roll my eyes. Slut? Really? That's what we're going with?

The tingling of the alcohol floats through my body, lightening my mood but somehow empowering me to get off my ass and climb my way out of the booth.

There's no way I'm going to miss out on this action, not when it's finally getting good.

I grip Dash's collar and pull him behind me, nestling him into the corner of the bar.

Four completely new demons appear from who knows where and attack Bo, dragging his attention away from Storm. He stumbles only slightly and regains his footing, ducking to kick the legs out from under one and punching his fist through the chest of another. He rips the demon's black heart out and squeezes until it turns to mush.

Storm lays at my feet, whimpering and bleeding out. If only I were the one to have done that to him. I guess carnage inflicted on his peers will have to suffice.

I latch onto one of the demons after Bo and thrust him to the side.

"Fucking bitch," the vampire-like creature spits.

I'll show him a bitch.

I spin on my left leg, circling my body and putting all my force into kicking him square in the jaw with my right foot.

He stumbles into a table, breaking it with his fall, and clutches his face. The demon spits a darkly discolored substance onto the floor. "I'll kill you for that."

I cup my fingers and motion for him to bring it, a devious grin no doubt caked on my face. This is the shit I live for.

He heaves his body at me, and despite his supernatural speed, I hop out of the way in time, sending him into an empty space, causing his frustration to rise even more.

I can't help but laugh at the pathetic attempt to subdue me.

"Oh, you think this is funny, do you?" He raises his upper lip, snarling and exposing his fangs, a bit of his own blood spattering out. His gaze flits to something behind me, and he dips his head barely enough to signal to whoever must be joining us.

Grabbing a knife off a nearby table, I secure it in my hand and spin out of his path once more. I shove a chair at him and scan to see who the newcomer might be.

Another demon, not one of these two, blasts me with a chair, pieces of the wooden thing splintering and flying all around. I stifle a groan at the impact and rotate quickly, shoving the blade into the creature's calf.

It cries out and drops to the floor, clutching the gushing wound left when I yank the blade out. I jerk my arm back and plunge the knife into its chest and dodge another chair from my vampire fight partner.

The thing explodes and I catch a rather large chunk of it as it flies past my head. I rise to my feet, sizing up both opponents and smirking at their failed attacks.

The entire tavern has erupted in chaos. Demons fight demons for no reason other than because they can. What started as a dispute at our table became a full brawl for the sake of drawing blood. I can't say I disagree with their ways, regardless of how senseless they may be. Especially when it's this damn fun.

Two more of their kind rush over behind them, making it a four-on-one battle.

I scan the floor, looking for other possible weapons and ways for me to get creative with ending their lives.

Bo's baggy shirt hangs from me like a loose nightgown, more blood speckled on it now than when he tossed it to me. Not that I imagine he'll mind—he's sort of disgusting either way. Something about it is incredibly infuriating, too.

Dash drops to my side and I almost stake him with the wood in my fist. His eyes go wide.

I want to say sorry, that I thought he was one of them, but the spell Wes has on me is still too strong.

The four vampires jump on us with haste, two on Dash, two on me.

Fuck. Not what I had bargained for. It was fine when it was my battle, but now that Dash is involved...

I latch onto mine while Dash uppercuts the fang-toothed creature in his grasp, its venomous teeth clanging together and its head snapping up violently. He ducks out of the way from the other one, sending a jab up its chin, too.

I blink a couple times, not sure if I'm seeing this correctly. That was a solid punch for a human, let alone on something with supernatural strength. Maybe Dash isn't so helpless after all.

"Are you fucking kidding me?" Wes calls out. He

slams his fist into the face of a man who swings at him first, knocking the guy to the floor with a thud. He shoves two more on his way into the anarchy.

Hissing draws my attention from the filthy bloodsuckers chomping at the bit to drain me.

Impatient little shits. I hike my leg up, kneeing the vamp straight in the groin, buckling him over. With the reinforced padding and armored additions to my clothing, there's no type of man that wouldn't hurt—demon or not.

"Bitch," the thing blurts out while clutching its groin.

Quickly, I grip a fistful of his hair and hold him in place, taking that same knee and jolting it up into his face this time.

The other vampire, clearly shocked at my ability to battle them with ease, stutters before deciding that grabbing my arm is the best idea. Exposing his fangs, he sinks them into the soft flesh, his venom stinging my skin and sending a burning sensation up into my chest.

He immediately withdraws, coughing and hacking up the blood he just drew. He drops to his knees, alongside his partner who is still trying to regain his composure.

I've been bit by various creatures in the past, can't say I've ever had that reaction.

The thing writhes in pain and claws at my ankle.

I kick it away, the same moment something tackles me from behind, knocking me to the ground.

This is usually where I mutter a few colorful words.

"Wren," Dash cries out from somewhere.

I crane my head to make sure he's okay, but the weight of the beast is too much. My body aches under the pressure, the air escaping my lungs and my chest unable to rise and refill. If I don't get this thing off me soon, it's going to fucking suffocate me. Sure would be nice to, I don't know, maybe ask for a little fucking assistance from the folks I came here with.

I've never had help before though, so why would I expect anything different here?

Hot breath nips at my neck and saliva dribbles out onto my cheek.

Did this thing just tackle me and fucking pass out?

That's when it dawns on me—the mass, the nasty breath, the motionless weight of it—this *thing* is a scurni. And yes, it did, in fact, just take a nap on my rather small frame.

The ogre-type creature might be large and strong, but it has goat-like tendencies where they faint when overexerted. Meaning, the chances of it crushing me are pretty high if I can't get it off before I run out of air.

I wiggle with all my might to press my palm flat against the debris-covered ground and strain to get this thing to budge. Pain shoots up my arm from the place that vampire had bitten me.

Great. Not only am I not operating at full strength, but that bite is hindering what little of my power still remains. The lack of air no doubt making the entire situation even worse. If it weren't for the armor encasing my body and holding the brunt of this beast's mass, I'd already be dead. And I will be soon if I don't figure this out.

Maybe dying isn't so bad. I mean, the likelihood of me making it out of the next few days is pretty slim, given the control Wes has over me and the mark on my neck left by the idiot who most definitely wants me dead. If it's not them that end my life, or the countless demons we'll encounter on our way, the guards at Rock Bridge will make a solid attempt at killing all of us on sight. If this first outing is any indication of the shit-storm we're bound to face, I'd wager to say none of us make it out alive.

But when have I ever gone down without a fight? And to die at the hands, or well, the massive weight of a scurni—doesn't seem like a very worthy death for an acclaimed warrior.

So, I do what I always do, I dig my heels in and don't give up.

One minute of self-pity is enough for this week.

I ignore the shooting pain in my arm and push again, rocking the beast ever so gently. Its weight heaves down on me with each movement, and the soft crunching coming from my armor alerts me to the ticking clock that remains. My gear can only hold on for so long, and then I'm a goner for sure. Without its assistance, this scurni will smash me like a bug.

I blink through my clouded vision and search for

anything that can be of use. I spot the metal leg of a nearby booth, welding securely into the floor. I reach for it, the cracking growing louder by the second. The battle between moving too quickly and not slow enough is a fine line I'm barely hanging onto.

My ears pop and are unable to make out the commotion around us. I have no idea if the vampires killed Dash, or if Wes and Bo are faring well in this fight. For all I know, they've finished and are sitting at the bar chugging their ale and toasting to finally getting rid of me for good. Maybe they're taking bets on how long until this thing flattens me like a pancake.

I extend my hand, my fingertips grazing the cold metal. I clench my jaw and muster all my willpower to go a little further. I wrap my aching grip around the thing and pull with everything I have.

The beast groans and shifts its position just enough to give me the chance to free part of my torso, the weight of it crushing the bottom half of my body.

"One, two, pull," someone shouts.

The beast's body rocks, and I free myself completely. My chest heaves with the ability to finally expand without the crushing weight of the ogre. But, with each breath, another sharp pain spikes through me. If it's not one thing, it's another. Regardless of the new source of agony, I latch onto the discarded blade under the booth and bring myself to my feet.

The scurni hitting the floor rattles the old tavern and sends a shiver up my spine.

"Holy shit, Wren," Dash rushes over to me, his hands hovering over my body as frantically as his gaze. "Are you...are you okay?"

I swallow and blink to clear my vision, settling my sights on Wes and Bo behind him.

Bo drops to his knee and drives a knife into the chest of the vampire who bit me, pulling it out and repeating the motion three times. Overkill for sure, but still satisfying all the same.

"We need to get out of here." Wes rushes over and grips my elbow.

I yank it away from him and stifle a wince at the swift motion. My entire body aches, from the top of my head to the tip of my toes. I guess that's what happens when a giant fucking beast takes a nap on top of you.

Couldn't that have happened to Bo instead? Not the smallest member of our little group.

"We can assess your wounds later, right now, we need to leave." Wes nods toward the door he disappeared through earlier. "This way."

Keeping the blade I had found only a moment ago, I cling it to my side and follow him through the remains of the fallen. Whimpers float through the space but I don't bother taking inventory of the casualties. I'm not too stupid to know I need to get the hell out of here.

"There," someone shouts. "The hunter is right there."

Fuck.

12

WES

Wren is in pain—I can feel it in my soul.

The second I scanned that tavern and couldn't find her, the world felt like it slipped from my grasp. My beast slaughtered every demon in our path between us and her. I had caught a glance of a sliver of her hair under that hideous ogre and immediately thought the worst. Bo helped me lift that thing off her, and the whole time, I feared that she was dead—that I had lost her forever.

The blasphemy of my emotions grows out of control with each passing moment. Even if she cannot be mine, the idea that I caused her death would be something I could not live with. Every moment she spends in our captivity is one more that I put her in danger. But we're all in too deep now. Bridges have been crossed that cannot be taken again and the only way we can go is forward.

Bo has marked her and he's made it known that he will not rid her of it until she follows through with her end of the bargain. A deal that puts all our lives at risk.

He won't even tell me the details—just that it can be done. I'm putting my faith in him that he's telling the truth, because if he isn't, that means I lied to Wren, and given her connection to my beast, that's a serious offense.

"Wes, hello, you fucking idiot." Bo shoves me and points toward the door we just ran through. "Catch the building on fire."

My gaze trails over Wren, then Dash, and Bo, confirming they're all on this side with me. I draw in a long breath and allow the heat to bubble to the surface, my skin warming and my hands glowing brighter and brighter. I thrust two fistfuls of flames at the tavern and scream a wave of inferno, making it impossible for anyone to safely pass through the way we came.

"Run," I yell once I've finished.

They all comply, not a word coming from any of them.

A few moments of our labored breaths pass, and I follow Bo into a cave-like dwelling on the side of a hill.

"We need a plan," he admits.

Wren, knife in her left hand, makes a fist with her right and slams it across my cheek. She drops the blade into the dirt and shoves me with what little strength she has left.

"What the fuck?" I rub my jaw.

Bo leans against the entrance and raises his shoulder when I glance at him.

Dash tries to reach out to her, but she shrugs him off and gives him a death stare.

Turning back to me, she grunts and points to her mouth.

"What?" I furrow my brow, and then my stomach sinks—the mystery unraveling in my mind. "You can speak."

"I fucking hate you."

My beast and I wince. "I'm aware." I would hate me, too. What a fucking fool I am for abusing the very power I didn't want to abuse. I didn't mean for the control I have over her to be so fucking literal. I just didn't want her to draw attention to herself in that tavern, not take away her ability to speak permanently. It's no wonder she didn't scream for help under the weight of that ogre.

That thought alone rips my heart in two.

"If you ever fucking do that again..." Wren clenches her jaw. "I will slit your throat while you're sleeping."

"I...I didn't mean to..."

"You knew exactly what you were doing." She turns towards the other guys. "I know a place. It's not far from here."

I shake my head. "No. Not happening."

"Why?" She barely faces me.

"Because I don't trust you."

"Great," she blurts out. "Because I don't trust you

either. But I don't intend on sitting out here in the open just waiting for who knows how many demons are after us. Do you have a better idea?"

"I'm with Birdie." Bo surprisingly adds in while keeping his gaze trained outside the pathetic covering. "No sense in letting them gain on us."

That traitorous demon is really starting to piss me off.

"You're bleeding," Dash says to Wren, reaching for her arm.

She pulls away. "I'm fine."

What little trust she had in Dash seems to have been erased, too. We're not even a full day into this journey and shit has already massively hit the fan. The whole point in going to Breckenridge was to secure transport to Rock Bridge. Prior to finding Frank, the guy who was going to help with transportation, the brawl broke out at the tavern. Meaning, not only did the plan fail, but now we have demons aware we're traveling with a hunter, and they're hot on our asses.

"Let me see it." I step toward her, knowing damn well that I can fix the problem with a few simple words. A skill only capable of being used in our *unique* situation.

She glares up at me. "Don't you fucking touch me."

"Ouch," Bo mutters.

"I can at least..." Dash pulls off his backpack and unzips it.

"I'm fine," Wren snaps at us. "How many times do I

have to tell you? I'm fucking fine." She snatches the knife she discarded and walks over to where Bo is standing. "We're leaving, you can come or don't, I don't care either way."

"But..." My statement falls flat when they leave.

How did I go from being in charge to being left behind? This was all supposed to be my plan, and now she's calling the shots. Someone who Bo wanted to slaughter, is leading him to who knows fucking where. And he's a willing participant.

After a few minutes, Dash falls back to walk alongside me.

If I weren't seeing it for myself, I'd never believe that Wren and Bo would be shoulder to shoulder, chatting like they weren't on opposite sides of a war.

Is he doing this to get at me? So I'll admit the truth about what happened? The reality that I refuse to believe myself. The one my beast keeps taunting me with every chance he gets.

"What's up with that?" Dash tips his head toward the same sight I'm struggling with.

I shrug and scan the surrounding area to make sure we're not being followed. "I don't know."

"Hey..." He lowers his voice. "Can we talk?"

I side-eye him. "About what?"

Dash scratches at his neck, clearly uncomfortable about whatever it is that's on his mind.

My beast stirs at the very idea of it all.

"Not now, Dash." I swallow down the rage that builds up.

"I..." He flits his gaze at her then at me. "I didn't know."

"Didn't know what?"

"That you...your beast..."

"It's not what you think," I snap at him. "You're mistaken." A blip of fire puffs out of my mouth and zips past Dash's face.

He ducks out of the way but not before it singes a bit of his hair. "Christ, Wes, you could have hit me with that."

"I'm sorry," I cover my mouth and shake my head. "I didn't mean to." I really didn't.

Dash sighs and walks away, muttering with each step. "I was just trying to apologize."

I'm left alone once more and wish I could separate myself from the intense emotions threatening to tear me apart. It's enough that I feel the way I do about Wren, but to let it come between me and my friends, that's another. I'd never hurt Dash on purpose. Bo, on the other hand, yeah, I'd cause him pain every day of the week, but because he can take it, and has supernatural healing powers. And obviously, because he deserves it. He's an asshole—an arrogant and self-centered demon.

And right now, he has a better relationship with Wren than I do.

How the fuck is any of this possible?

When my beast locked its sights on her and refused to leave her behind in that building, I knew I had to come up with a plan. I would use the excuse that she could help us get our people back and in exchange, I could help her stay alive. The thought of the alternative was not an option. I would not allow her to die. I guess I didn't exactly think the entire thing through. I was a fool to assume I could control my beastly side. That in this entire lifetime spent with him, I had gained some kind of authority.

No, the moment he claimed her, I was a goner.

Not only does he want her, but he needs her, like the breath in his fucking lungs. The breath in mine—because he and I are one and the same. And for every bit of desire he has for her, so do I. That longing to be near her, to brush the hair from her face, to take away all her pain and give her everything she could ever ask for—I need that as much as he does. I shouldn't, he shouldn't, but we do, and there's not a damn thing I can do to change it.

The universe already decided it long before I had any say in the matter.

My fated mate—a fucking demon hunter.

13

WREN

I hurt all over. Each step is a heavy rippling wave of pain coursing through me, but every inch brings me a little closer to a temporary haven.

One of my safe houses, tucked in the woods, warded similarly to how the guys had their cabin, only with running water and more than a deflated cot to sleep in. It isn't much, but it will provide us some shelter to regroup and figure out our next move.

I'm running on pure adrenaline at this point—a mixture of the high from the demon fight and the anger I have toward Wes.

How dare he compel me not to speak. And then pout like a baby when I say I don't trust him. Why should I? Not when he doesn't bother giving me the same courtesy. I could have run on numerous occasions, and yet I haven't. I could have killed every one of them, and yet, they're all still standing, even thanks to me saving their asses. I'm bringing them to a place I seek refuge, which is absolutely not something I ever thought I'd do, considering they're quite literally the enemy, and still, that's not enough.

Doesn't he realize that I intend on holding up my end of the deal? I need the cure of the alpha bite, and the only way to get it is to see this thing through. Unless they change their mind, or I find out they're lying, I'm very much getting them to Rock Bridge.

The puncture wounds on my forearm burn, no doubt having some kind of weird reaction to the alpha venom that was already in my system. I can only imagine that's what caused the vampire to stop and vomit up my blood. Between that and the giant who nearly crushed me to death, I grow weary of how much longer I have before my body decides it's going to give out. I want to stop, catch my breath, and rest a little, but if I succumb to the darkness tugging at my consciousness, there's no telling what kind of trouble Wes will get us into.

"It's just..." I point through the thick brush. "Up ahead."

"You sure it's safe?" Bo asks me.

"Promise," I reply, the word barely a whisper on my lips.

"You okay?" Bo slows his pace to match mine. "You don't look so good."

"For hating me, you sure do care a lot."

Bo rolls his dark eyes, but there's a bit of playfulness

there that's new. He shoves a large branch aside and lets me walk ahead of him.

The murky night sky barely provides enough light to see where we're going, but home calls to me like the beacon on my neck does to demons. We're so close I can almost smell the lavender hanging in my kitchen and the eucalyptus in my shower.

I dig my heels in to climb up the final incline to my sanctuary. My foot catches on a rock, twisting my ankle and sending me backward.

Bo steadies me with his hand on my lower back. "Not trying to cop a feel."

"Uh huh, sure." I regain my footing, desperately ignoring the new blip of pain. Hasn't my body already had enough for one day?

"You good?" Bo asks when I don't continue.

Dizziness takes hold and it's everything I can do to stay upright.

"What's going on up there?" Wes asks from his spot in the back.

"I'm fine," I tell them. The same two words I've used over and over couldn't be further from the truth. I feel like shit. Like I've been crushed by a giant ogre and bitten by a vampire, and then hiked through the forest for a couple hours.

Oh wait, I have.

Bo steps up and cowers beside me. He takes one look at my face and then turns his back to me, still in the crouched position. "Climb on."

I blink at his bare skin. "What?"

He reaches behind, grabbing my hand and tugging me toward him. "Hop on, Birdie."

He can't be serious.

"I'm serious, get on. Hurry up before I change my mind." He brings my hand onto his shoulder and pulls me up with ease.

I reposition myself and wrap my arms around his neck, and my legs around his waist. Warmth flows through me at the close contact and my body thanks me for the reprieve. "You better not drop me."

Bo chuckles. "Don't tempt me."

"What the..." Wes mutters.

"She hurt her ankle, calm your tits, beast boy." Bo strolls up the hill at a much quicker pace than I was walking with ease, alerting me that I was holding us up from getting to safety.

We arrive at the top and I point the direction I want Bo to go.

"Uh, Birdie, are you sure you know where you're going?" Bo hesitantly walks toward what he assumes is nothing. "You're not delusional, are you? Wes is going to have my ass if he was right all along."

I mutter the incantation to myself to give the guys the same view that I have.

"Oh." Bo tenses for a second at the sudden change in scenery, and then briskly continues.

One of the perks I have from being a hunter—my safe houses are spelled so no one can access them without my consent. The few words I whispered give these three that ability. Here's to hoping I don't come to regret that decision.

"You can let me down now," I tell Bo once we're within a few yards of the porch.

He remains in motion, not stopping until he arrives at the small house. He turns and sets me down onto the wooden exterior.

I hobble over to the door, relief flooding through me when I grip the handle. It's only temporary, but it feels good to be somewhere familiar. Somewhere safe.

"Damn, Birdie, this place is nice." Bo climbs up behind me, pressing his arm above me and leaning against the side of the building. His scent floats down to me, and for the first time since we've met, I'm not utterly repulsed by it.

My head spins, the mixture of his venom and the vampires running through my veins does me no favors.

I stumble and reach for anything to steady myself.

"Whoa there." Bo places his large hand on my back.

Wes growls and hops onto the porch with us. He pulls Bo away. "Why are you so handsy all of a sudden? Did you forget you want her dead?"

"You're acting like children." I turn, but too quickly, causing my vision to blur that much more. I fall forward, everything going black as hands from each direction catch me from hitting the ground.

~

I wake sometime later, abruptly, sitting straight up and gasping for breath. I blink a few times, taking in the sights of my bare bedroom. I clutch my chest, my gaze trailing down to see that the puncture wound on my arm is gone, and the blood has been wiped away.

Wes, no doubt, doing the thing I asked him not to.

Burning wood crackles from the fireplace in the corner, and a small piece breaks off and falls to the side, a bit of smoke billowing up and away. The darkness of night through the window means I haven't been asleep too long.

The ache in my body tells me that Wes only healed *some* of my wounds, not all of them. Probably in his attempt to keep me weak and under his thumb. That bastard.

Hushed whispers bring my attention outside my closed-off room. I hold my breath and strain to hear what it is they think they're being secretive about.

"I told you, Wes, there is one." Bo pauses. "But you'll never let it happen."

"Why? Tell me what it is, and I'll decide for myself." Wes replies.

"Your mutt can't handle it."

"Don't act like you know what you're talking about."

"I see the way you look at her. It's obvious to everyone but you, and you're the idiot trying to ignore what nature has already commanded."

What the fuck is he talking about?

"I said *tell me*." A quiet but guttural growl follows Wes's words.

"See, right there. Why else would you be so defensive of a hunter if you weren't—."

"If you so much as finish that sentence, I will set you on fire."

"You're only continuing to convince me of what I already know."

I rack my brain to try to figure out what it is that they could be referring to. Wes has been nothing but evasive and weird since I met him, despite him randomly saving my life. Still, none of what they're saying adds up.

"Don't worry, once I tell her how the cure works," Bo adds, "she'll run for the hills. No way she'll go through with it either."

That's what this is all about? The fucking cure? The thing I've been using as motivation to go along with this entire stupid plan. The only reason I'm entertaining their idiocracy is something Bo is convinced I'll never do anyway.

Then what's the fucking point? Why risk my life to save more of their kind if there's nothing in it for me? I should have known these demons would bring me only disappointment and regret.

The firelight reflects off the knife sitting next to me on my bed, leading to countless ideas that pop across my mind. I could go out there, slice each one of their throats and be done with it. I could consume their souls and become a stronger version of myself, more powerful than ever before with their rare and mysterious energy. I could use it to slit my own throat and end the torment that will no doubt haunt me for the rest of my existence.

Instead, I grip the handle of the knife and carefully creep out of my bed, paying special attention to every creak I may cause. I tiptoe across the small space and as quietly as possible, lift the hatch on the window and tug it open. I eye the door and when I'm certain they haven't heard a peep, I climb out the opening and jump onto the ground. My feet land with a soft thud on the grassy surface and without another thought, I take off through the forest behind my house.

It's not much of a plan, and with the beacon on my neck, I can't imagine I'll get far, but considering I've been stuck with these fucking assholes for days, I need a moment to myself to process what the fuck I'm going to do with this new information.

I breathe in the night air and allow it to soak into my lungs. A light fog litters the ground and provides for an eerie yet calming stroll. Glancing over my shoulder, I exhale as the building grows smaller with each step away from it. My heart constricts at the sudden emptiness I feel without them around. What a strange immediate thought.

This whole time I've been dying to get away, and now that I am, I find myself unsure of quite literally everything. Maybe it's the mark on my neck causing me not to think clearly, or perhaps Wes has me under some kind of mind control spell again.

Either way, nothing makes sense at all.

Why wouldn't I take the cure? What could possibly be so fucking bad that I would refuse to do it? That Wes and his *mutt,* as Bo calls it, would disallow it from happening. Wes is the one who used the cure as a bargaining chip; why wouldn't he be a little more confident he could follow through with his end of the deal? Unless he never intended on delivering on his promise.

All of that aside, I still haven't figured out the answers to any of the other questions nagging at me. Like why my superiors failed to mention that Wes was anything other than some random demon. They played it off like he would be an easy target, and here I am, days into being around him and I'm no closer to determining what kind of powerful creature he is. Not to mention the fact that he's buds with an alpha and has taken a human under his wing to care for. None of that is typical demon behavior and goes against everything I've ever been told and conditioned to believe.

Why would they withhold vital information that could easily put my life in danger?

I get that I'm a soldier in this war, but I was under the impression I was valued and respected enough to get that kind of insider information.

No, I'm just a disposable grunt doing the work they aren't willing to do.

My neck burns the further I get away from Bo. That

stupid fucking marker getting close to alerting any nearby demon of my whereabouts. I sigh, stopping my impromptu walk, and lean against a large tree. The ache in my ribs throbs through me at the pressure of my back on the hard surface.

Couldn't Wes have just healed those, too? Or maybe he wasn't aware of them since they're not visible. I guess I could give him a few brownie points for not looking where he shouldn't be while I'm unconscious.

A familiar sensation flutters in my chest. My warrior alert system kicking in. Something that's been on the fritz since these three came into my life. I disregard it at first. But it lingers there unwilling to dissipate.

A scream follows, making its way through the forest and slamming me in the gut.

An all too human sound.

Not wasting another second, I kick off the trunk of the tree and take off into a sprint. I push my legs harder to move quickly over the patchy terrain. I hop over a fallen log and burst straight through a bush, not a care in the world about the briars that plunge themselves into my flesh or the rippling of pain from my broken and bruised ribs.

The closer I get, the deeper the thought that I won't make it there in time. I push myself harder, drawing the blade from where I had sheathed in my waistband as I run onto a boulder, leaping through the air and landing within arm's reach of a demon. I shove the knife into its back, yanking it out in one swift motion, and turn to the others.

My fears are confirmed when my eyes settle on Dash, being held captive by a wendigo easily twice his size. The one from the fucking tavern.

Dash screams again, but the thing shoves its filthy hand over his mouth to muffle the sound.

Anger rises up within me. A possessiveness I will add to the list of things I cannot explain.

A swarm of darkness appears from the trees behind the wendigo. Partially shifted wolves, drakka, and beasts I cannot identify rush past them and unleash themselves on me.

I steady my footing and eye each of them, only one weapon in my grasp and a dozen demons that need to die.

The first, a vampire-looking thing, uses its supernatural speed to advance on me, but not before I pivot and shove the knife into its heart. Another two try their luck, only to meet the same fate. I spin and duck and use every single fight I've been in and ounce of training I've ever received to allow my body to do what it does best—destroy.

In the blur of the chaos, two dominant figures appear, one glowing bright red, engulfing everything he sets his sights on into flames, and the other, snapping neck after neck.

A sense of hope reverberates through me.

But we all know, hope is a fickle bitch.

I shift toward the wendigo holding onto Dash, ready to take matters into my own hands. But instead of releasing him and fighting someone on his own level, he does the unthinkable.

With a solid and swift motion, the ungodly beast places a hand on the front and back of Dash's head, his ginger locks flowing through the demon's fingers as his neck is abruptly snapped.

For a split moment, Dash and I lock eyes, a million words unspoken between us. And like the life is being sucked from the both of us, his limp body drops to the cold, hard ground.

"No!" I scream, but it's no use. The worst has already happened.

And there is not a damn thing I can do about it.

Dash is dead, and it's all my fault.

14
WREN

The wendigo takes my momentary surprise as its excuse to retreat into the shadows of night. Fighting me was one thing, but upon Wes and Bo arriving, it knew the chances of it surviving were slim to none.

I scuttle across the ground over to where Dash's body remains.

Unmoving. Unresponsive. Dead.

I brush the golden locks from his forehead. "No," I whisper. This can't be happening.

Out of the corner of my eye, I spot Wes and Bo finishing off the last of the wolves that stuck around. I hop up and rush over to them.

"Heal him," I yell at Wes. "Do something."

He shakes his head, his brows furrowed. "It doesn't work like that."

"Why?" I point to my leg and then my arm. "You did

it for me. Do it for him." I reach for his arm and tug at him.

He yanks himself free. "Wren, stop."

Bo crouches next to Dash's lifeless body and runs his fingers over Dash's eyes to close his lids. "He's gone."

"No." I refuse to believe that. Because if I do, then I'll have to come to terms with the fact that it was my fault. That Dash is dead because of me. And that's not a reality I'm ready to face just yet. I drop to the ground and lightly smack Dash's expressionless face. "Wake up, Dash. Come on, wake up." I pinch his nose and open his mouth, breathing what life I have into him and hoping like hell it works. Pressing my hands into a ball, I push on his chest, pumping him the way I was taught all those years ago when I was a child. If only I had paid more attention, I'd be more confident in knowing what I was doing. I simply go through the motions as best as I can remember. "Dash, please."

Minutes pass of my failed attempt at bringing him back. Wes and Bo remain quiet while they watch me with pity. I don't even know why I do it, knowing in my gut that his injuries are far more serious than breathing life back into him.

Unwilling tears roll down my cheeks at the loss of a man I barely knew, but knew well enough that he didn't deserve what this life gave him. This world. It was far too cruel for someone like Dash.

"There has to be something," I mutter.

Bo kneels next to me and places his hand on my shoulder. "Wren, he's gone."

My name, he used my name. Which can only mean that he's not trying to tease me, or play coy, he wants me to understand that this innocent man is truly dead.

I blink up at Wes. "Why can't you heal him? Tell me." I stand and wipe at my cheeks. "And why won't I take the cure?" I look between Wes and Bo, desperate for answers to any of my questions.

When they don't speak, I raise my voice. "I deserve the truth."

Bo scratches his neck and glances at Wes. "Dude, you should take the lead on this one."

Wes runs his hand through his hair. "I...I don't know where to start."

"What's the point then? Huh? If you won't tell me. What reason could you possibly have to keep things from me? Have I not proven myself trustworthy? I agreed to this fucking mission, and I've let you recklessly endanger all of our lives, and for what?"

"You wouldn't understand." Wes averts his gaze.

I step toward him and shove his chest. "Then make me understand." I turn toward Bo, pointing my finger at him. "You're just as guilty so knock that smug look off your face." I yank the knife tucked into his waistband out. "Fine, if you two don't want to talk." I flip the blade so it presses into the exposed skin right near my heart.

Both of them lurch forward but I anticipate it and

match their stride the opposite way. "Don't you fucking come any closer." I push the blade in, drawing a bit of blood that trickles down my breast. "If you won't give me answers…"

I never really anticipated my death coming at my own hands but with the way things have been going lately, I don't think I'm at all surprised. Who better to end my life than myself? At least I will go down on my own terms. Not because of some demon.

I'm exhausted. Both mentally and physically. I'm not a quitter—I just don't really want to go on. I mean, what's the fucking point when quite literally nothing makes sense? My entire life hinges upon lies and deception and I find it difficult to know what to believe in. What to trust. It's hard to put faith in my own thoughts when even they betray me.

I glance down at my feet, where Dash's body remains.

"Wren, can you…" Wes pleads.

How does he not realize he holds all the cards right now? If he would be honest with me, maybe I'd put down the knife.

A crackling sound comes from Dash, stealing my attention from Wes's concern-riddled face. It's strange really, to witness two incredibly powerful creatures actually show worry at my dramatic display. Why would they care if I end my life or not?

Oh, wait, they can't continue to use me as leverage. That's why.

Dash's lifeless body starts to smoke, then catches fire.

Panicked, I look at Wes, but there is no sign of his beast side showing through. And if Wes didn't cause the fire, then what did?

Dash burns for an agonizing second, his entire body going up in flames.

"Is that supposed to happen to humans in this realm?" I watch in horror as Dash disappears in the blaze.

The flames burn out and a solid shell encases where he once was.

"I don't...I don't think so." Wes appears at my side.

Bo snatches the knife from my slack hand, offering me an apologetic shrug at having seized the distracted opportunity. He returns his attention to Dash with the rest of us.

The hardened tomb-like thing cracks and a hand reaches through.

Dash—unharmed, and somehow alive breaks through the surface, the encasement breaking all around him.

"How is this possible? You're...you were..." But my words continue to fail me.

"A phoenix," Bo declares, reaching down to help Dash to his feet. "My boy is a fucking phoenix."

It's no wonder I couldn't sense a demonic aura on Dash—because he has none. His magic is pure, untainted, and unlike anything I've ever come across. In all my years, I've never heard of a phoenix being in our realm. And if I'm not mistaken, their kind is almost completely extinct, making the story of why no one came for Dash all that much more credible.

Without thinking, I wrap my arms around Dash's neck and pull him to me.

Too damn slowly, he latches onto my waist and picks me off the ground.

"I thought you were dead." I weep into his neck.

He breathes me in and squeezes me tightly. "I think I was."

Dash sets me to the ground, and I study him over, not a scratch or ginger hair out of place. Just that adorable grin and those baby blue eyes.

"What did I miss?" He asks us.

Bo is the first to speak up, because why wouldn't he want to hear himself talk? "Birdie here was about to off herself."

I narrow my gaze and glare at him.

"What? Why?" Dash scans all around us, no doubt taking in all the dead demon bodies around us.

Bo shrugs. "Must really be into that whole Romeo and Juliet thing."

"What's the last thing you remember?" Wes ignores Bo's remarks and focuses on Dash.

Dash puts his finger to his chin. "I...um...I came out here." He looks to me. "To find you." Then he motions to the massacre. "And I'm pretty sure that big scary thing from the tavern was here. You know, that beast with the antlers and the skull and stuff." He shakes his head. "Creepy son of a bitch."

"Wendigo," the rest of us say in unison.

"Yeah, that." He scans the crowd again. "Um…"

"It got away," I tell him. I should have gone after it, but I was a bit more concerned with Dash being dead. Mark my words, one way or another, I will hunt it down and make it suffer for what it put us all through.

I shift my focus to these men around me. Wes—the enigma who is more powerful than Bo, the alpha of alphas, and Dash, a complete rarity to the supernatural world—a freaking phoenix who rises from its own ashes upon its death. All three are unheard of, and here I am, in the presence of each one of them.

"We can worry about that later," Wes says. "We shouldn't stay out here in the open much longer."

I take a step but then realize none of the things I asked were answered. I glue my feet in place. "I'm not moving until *someone* tells me *something*."

Dash widens his stare. "Um." He glances between us. "I'm a phoenix?" He draws out the last word and squints a bit.

I let out an exasperated breath. "Not you." I pat his shoulder and let the gratefulness of his continued existence calm me.

Bo points to Wes. "He's in love with you."

I swallow, then blink a few times. "I'm sorry, *what*?" Crossing my arms over my chest, I wait for some kind of explanation. Is this some ruse to get me to stop asking questions? I jut out my hip. "Is this true?" I stare directly at Wes, whose face reddens, but not because of his beastly abilities.

"I fucking knew it," Dash adds.

"Knew what?" Why can't these guys just fucking answer me?

"That's why your beast has been pissed at me. Because I slept with her." Dash nods his head like all the pieces are starting to fall into place.

Must be fucking nice not being in the dark.

I slap his arm lightly. "A little discretion, if you will."

A growl ripples out of Wes and a burst of fire follows the sound.

I grab Dash out of the line of fire but not before the flame licks at my skin.

"What the fuck, Wes." Bo shoves Wes with force, knocking him off his feet. "You could have hurt her."

"Um, hello?" I point to my blistered arm and then press my hand to it even though that's probably not the ideal thing to do. "And what do you care? Don't you want me dead anyway?"

Dash steps in front of me like he's going to protect me.

I smile at the thoughtful and misplaced gesture.

"Don't you think if I wanted you dead, that you'd already be dead?" Bo rolls his eyes.

"This is all your fault," Wes slams his palms into Bo, pushing him the same way Bo had done to him. "If you hadn't started that fucking fight at the tavern, we wouldn't be in this mess."

"Well, *excuse me* for defending her fucking honor," Bo blurts out.

All three of us gawk at him.

"What?" He throws his hands up. "The dude was out of line. He had it coming."

"Wait, you're telling me you beat the shit out of that demon because he was *hitting* on me?" Am I hearing this correctly or did Bo actually do a gentlemanly thing?

"He said he'd wait his turn, as if you were some piece of meat to go around." Bo continues to surprise me with each word.

"Oh," Wes mumbles. He extends his hand. "Well, then. Thank you."

"Thank you?" I retort. "You're *thanking* him?"

The two of them shake hands and a sort of unspoken understanding falls between them.

I shake my head. "Whatever." I storm off, heading back in the direction of my house. One thing is for sure, we shouldn't be out here any longer. There's no sense in waiting for more demons to attack us while we're all still reeling from our last battle. At least my place is warded from that kind of thing while we regroup.

And regroup is definitely what we need to do after *all* that just happened.

I stomp my feet each step of the way, the guys hot on my trail as they follow me without saying anything.

Of course they won't. They're all about keeping secrets and being weirdos who I'll never seem to understand.

My body continues to ache, and now my head decides to join in on the fun from the tears I had shed at thinking Dash had died. My forearm stings from the burn of Wes's flame, and my mouth feels like it's full of cotton. I need a damn drink—a stiff one, that's for sure.

I burst through the threshold of my house, the door open upon my arrival, no doubt a result of Wes and Bo rushing out at hearing the same scream I had heard from Dash. I go straight to my kitchen, and pull a bottle of the strongest whiskey I have available off the top shelf. I pour myself a thick helping of it, and down the contents in one fell swoop.

The guys hover inside, but near the exit, looking all like they might flee at the slightest confrontation.

"You." I point to Wes. "You are going to get us all killed if you don't get yourself under control. And that thing, I know you know what I'm talking about. If you do it again, I will fucking castrate you."

Wes swallows roughly and nods. "I understand."

"You." I turn my attention to Bo. "Is there a cure or not? Don't fucking lie to me."

"There is." Bo steps into the kitchen and takes the bottle from my hand and pours himself a glass. "But you're not going to like it."

I glance up at him. "Do any of you have to die?"

"What?" Bo scrunches his brows together. "No. Of course not."

"Okay, well whatever it is. I'm sure it'll be fine. We can cross that bridge when we get there."

"You." I focus on Dash.

"Yes, ma'am?"

"Try not to die again, that was unpleasant."

Dash blushes and rubs at his neck. "You care if I die?"

"Is it not obvious?"

"I just..." He tugs at his bottom lip with his teeth. "I wasn't sure. I sort of misjudged you and thought you were going to kill Bo, you know, with the whole knife throwing thing."

"Hell, even I wasn't totally convinced I wasn't going to kill him, until I didn't." I look over at the arrogant asshole who is currently downing all my booze.

From the moment I saw him—sensed him—I wanted to end his life. It was the hunter nature kicking in like it always has. I see the enemy, I eliminate it. And Bo, he is very much the enemy in every sense of the term. But strangely enough, he's grown on me. How? I have no fucking idea. Maybe it's the subtle kindness he exudes, like making sure Dash stays behind him during battle, breaking off chunks of bread for us before allowing himself the pleasure of indulging, and fighting off that ignorant demon who insisted on insulting me. I recall the satisfaction on his face when he smashed that vampire's heart in his hand, and stabbing the one who had bitten me, and the high-five he gave me when we tag-teamed destroying those demons together. Or maybe it was the innocent piggyback ride when I twisted my ankle.

It's a collective of things, really, all adding up to the fact that I don't hate him as much as I once did.

Plus, I mean, if we're being honest, he's a total smoke show with that bad boy dark vibe about him and his rock-hard, chiseled body. He even has the long, jet-black hair totally working in his favor thing going on. His looks alone are a convincing argument to keep him around.

"So, you're not mad at me?" Dash asks while hesitantly stepping closer.

"No." I shake my head and extend my refilled cup to him. "You want a drink?"

Wes does that thing he always does, growls a bit from his chest.

"Okay, *that*. Whatever *that* was. Has to stop." I glare at him.

He clears his throat. "I'm sorry, I didn't mean to."

"Then who did? Explain to me what's happening so I understand." When he doesn't say a word, I press my hand to Bo's shoulder. "Does this make you angry?" I mouth to Bo, "Just go with it."

He grins and winks at me, grabbing me by the waist and tugging me toward him. "With pleasure," Bo whispers into my ear.

I turn, pressing my ass up against Bo and reaching for Dash, who goes along with the plan without a second thought.

Dash cups my face in his palms and runs his thumb along my cheek, his gaze trailing down to my lips. "May I?"

I reply by pressing my mouth to his, but we're soon interrupted by the fiery inferno that engulfs Wes upon our embrace.

"Shit, fuck." Wes flings his arms like he's trying to put himself out. "I…" He continues to shake them.

I can't help but laugh at the sight of such a commanding beast struggling to gain control of his power. "You better put that out before you burn my house down."

Wes sighs and a blip of fire rolls out of his mouth. "I'm fucking trying."

I step away from Bo and Dash and approach Wes. "Hey," I say softly.

He meets my gaze, and there's something painful about the way he looks at me. A struggle I'm not sure I could ever understand hidden behind his eyes. "I never asked for this."

"Asked for what?" I continue toward him as his flames die down.

"Careful, Birdie," Bo calls out from behind me.

I ignore his warning, knowing damn well I was ready to drive a knife through my heart not too long ago because of their lack of answers. What's the worst that could happen now? Wes catches me on fire? I could think of worse ways to die.

I glance over my shoulder. "Could you two give us a minute?"

They nod and shuffle out of the room, through the front door.

"We'll be right out here if you need us," Bo mumbles on his way out.

I reach for Wes, his hand glowing and then returning to normal. "Come." I lead him into the small sitting area and drag him onto the couch beside me. Maybe if I get him more comfortable, he'll spill whatever it is that's going on with him.

Wes stiffly complies, his body facing away from me. "This isn't a good idea."

I grab his knee and pivot him in my direction while pulling my own legs onto the couch.

"Why?" I prop my arm up on the back of the couch and rest my head on it.

His gaze shifts to where he had burnt me.

"I'm fine, really." Between all the other injuries I've sustained the past few days, that one is just a small drop in the barrel.

"Okay, if you won't talk, then I will. Correct me if I'm wrong." I clear my throat. "So, I was ordered to kill you, obviously. And I majorly failed at that. Which isn't something I ever do, making this an entirely new situation for me. Instead of you letting me die there alone, or finishing me off, you bring me back to your place, and nurse me back to moderate health, and then decide I'll be useful to you in this mission of saving your friends from Rock Bridge. But here's the thing I'm unsure of. Did the idea to use me come before or after you saved me from that building?" I leave out the part about why I didn't succeed in killing him. That, the moment I locked eyes with him across that building, something fluttered in my chest that I haven't been able to make sense of no matter how hard I try. Something I've continued to ignore each time he's near.

Wes clenches his jaw.

I continue, "You show signs of jealousy when Bo or Dash get close to me. You have been a jerk to Dash since you realized we had sex. And your entire body was set on fire a few minutes ago. Bo blurted out that you're in love with me, but that doesn't really add up considering aside from the time you kept me from freezing to death in my sleep, you do pretty much everything you can to stay away from me, like I have the fucking plague."

Finally, his lips part. "I don't think you have the plague."

"Then what, are you into Bo or Dash, and you don't want me near them?"

His dark eyes go wide. "You think I'm...?" Wes shakes his head and chuckles. "No."

"Then what? Why do you refuse to tell me the truth?"

"Because I can't change it, no matter how hard I try. And if I say it out loud, then..."

"Change what?"

"Fate."

I blink at him, still not following where he's going with this. What does fate have to do with anything?

"My hound..." Wes takes a steady breath in and then meets my gaze. "Has claimed you as his mate."

Finally, it's my turn to be speechless.

His *hound*? Mate? How is that possible? I'm a hunter. Why would he want me out of everyone else he could choose from?

"Say something, please." Wes swallows like it causes him pain.

"I didn't expect that." But it makes sense of the way he's acted. And the sensation rippling through my chest when I saw him. It wasn't *just* his hound that felt the connection, but me, too. I've never heard of such a thing happening to a hunter before.

Something he had said sticks out in my head. It takes the shape of an ugly insecurity rooting in place.

"Wait, you...you don't want it? The fated mate bond?"

He said it himself that he can't change it, meaning that he would if he could. He's definitely done what he can to refrain from acting upon it. Is he repulsed that his hound would pick me?

"It's unnatural." Wes points to me. "You're a hunter." And then to himself. "And I'm...your target."

I nod slowly and lower my gaze. "I understand."

Wes reaches forward and tips my chin up. "I didn't say I didn't want it."

I ask the question I shouldn't. "Then what do you want?"

He sighs and skims the side of my cheek with his knuckles. "You."

That simple word is enough validation to give me an overwhelming amount of confidence and send me climbing across the couch and onto his lap. I straddle his legs and press my palms to his broad chest.

"What are you doing?" He stares at me with wild eyes.

"Shut up and kiss me."

His hardened expression softens, and he runs his hands up my neck and weaves his fingers into my hair, tugging me down and pressing my mouth to his. There's nothing gentle about it, just a purely passionate moment that took entirely too long to come to fruition.

Wes's warm tongue skims itself along mine and a low groan rumbles out of his chest.

I grip my fingers in his thick, dark hair, and run my nails against his scalp. My body melts into his, becoming this over clothed unit that can't seem to get close enough. I've never lusted for a being more in my entire life, and a month ago, if someone would have told me who it would be with, I'd slit their throat just for making such a wild and outlandish statement. Now, I can't imagine it any other way.

The front door bursts open and Wes pulls himself free from my kiss, apparently having more self-control than I do.

"Sorry to break up what looks like a great time," Bo apologizes. "But there's howling outside, which probably means we shouldn't be out there as the welcome party to whatever demons are searching for us."

"Right, yeah." I climb off Wes and pat my, no doubt, unruly hair down. I wipe at my moistened lips and fight the urge to say fuck it all and climb back on top of Wes, not a care in the world who might bear witness to us both finally giving in to our carnal desires.

15

BO

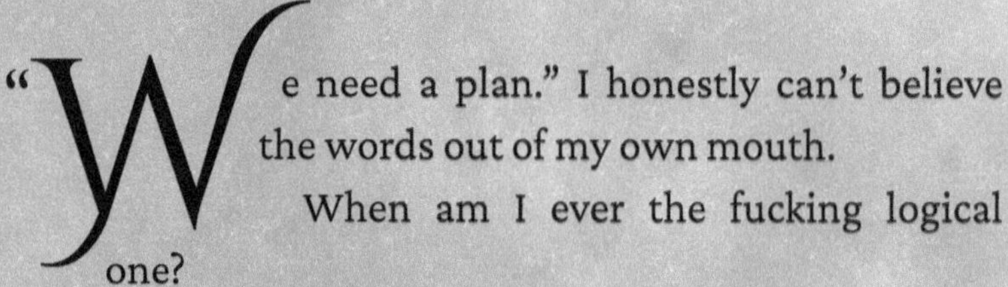

"We need a plan." I honestly can't believe the words out of my own mouth.

When am I ever the fucking logical one?

I'm used to living my life on the run, constantly wondering where my next meal might come from or who's plotting to try their hand at killing me.

But now, everything has changed.

I should've realized it sooner. Like the moment I acted on impulse and tasted her decadent blood in my mouth, or when the craving for death nearly overcame me when that demon wouldn't leave her alone. The satisfaction of blasting my fist through that vampire's chest and ripping out its heart should have alerted me to the shift in dynamic, but I was just as much an ignorant fool as the rest of us. None of that matters though if we don't stay alive.

A wendigo has set its sights on us, and has no intention of letting us go until we're dead.

And the tricky thing about those creatures is, even if we manage to kill the bastard, he's already shared the intention with his many followers, making survival in this realm that much more difficult.

Fucking yay.

If things weren't hard enough with the hunters, now the demons are after us, too.

"A plan." Wren adjusts her armor. "Get inside." She mutters something under her breath. "I've spelled the house to be concealed from anyone other than us. But there's no telling how long it will hold if they have a witch on their side."

Wes clears his throat and straightens up on the couch.

From the smug look on his face, he must have finally told her the fucking truth. That his hound has a perma-boner for her. And if I'm not mistaken, the news must have been well received since I caught her straddling him in a pretty heated make-out session. I could smell her lust before I stepped foot through the front door.

Maybe shit will be less awkward now that the truth is out.

Either way, his bond to her is unimportant in the grand scheme of things.

"Someone want to tell me why this feels much more dire than it typically does?" Dash glances between us for answers. "I mean, don't get me wrong, I'm getting used to this way of life, but this feels...I don't know...bigger."

"Wendigos don't like to lose," I tell him. "I'm assuming when they found out she was a hunter back at the tavern, the dude volunteered to take us out. Since he was unsuccessful, and we ran him off, he's probably recruited all of his little minions to assist in finishing the job."

Dash nods. "So, it's like, personal."

"Yep. And he'll stop at nothing to make sure it happens."

"Cool."

"It's nothing we can't handle." Wren strolls over to the kitchen and stands on her tiptoes to reach into a cabinet. She pulls out a loaf of bread and sets it on the counter, then pulls out a large platter and plops the bread onto it. Digging through her fridge, she drags out a few hunks of cheese. She snatches an apple out of the wicker basket, sniffs it, and takes a bite. Satisfied, she places three more on the tray and carries it over. "Eat."

I study her every move and wonder where she gets all that confidence from. She's tiny, and somehow, manages to kick major ass.

Wren breaks off a chunk of the bread and tosses it to me. "I said eat."

I catch it and grin. A girl who knows the way to my heart is through my stomach. Is there anything she isn't capable of?

And that's if she even considered me that way. There's no denying shit has been rocky between us from the start. The whole being complete enemies and all, and the numerous times I've threatened her life, and the mark I put on her neck like the arrogant asshole I am. I wouldn't like me if I were her.

"Demon zones are off-limits then." Wren settles into her spot on the couch.

Dash follows her over and sits in the chair next to her, while Wes remains disheveled and flustered.

I drag a chair from the dining table over and flip it to sit in it backward. I rest my arm on the back of it and chew the bread she gave me. "Obviously. Why? What did you have in mind?"

"What if we try a different approach?" Wren reaches for the apple she had already taken a bite of and nibbles off another piece of it. She wipes at her lip with her thumb and sucks the juice off.

Fuck. That was hot.

"Like what?" Wes snaps out of his stupor and goes into strategy mode, something I find myself struggling with at the moment.

It's easy to get distracted with Wren looking the way she does.

And the recollection of her ass pressed up against my groin while she was trying to make Wes jealous was pure fucking bliss.

"Do you trust me?" She flits her gaze between me and him.

"Of course," Dash answers for us, even though I don't think she was considering him as part of the equation. That idiot has been wrapped around her finger since she abruptly stepped foot into our lives.

And that lucky bastard has already gotten a taste of what it's like to be with her.

"The shortest route between here and Rock Bridge is hunter territory. It's a straight shot that will lead us right there with minimal chance of them following us. They'd have to circle around unless they're willing to go headfirst into the danger zone. I know the terrain like the back of my hand. From there, I have another safe house that's not too far where we can regroup and figure out what to do next once we rescue your people."

She's still willing to see our plan through, after everything that's happened?

"Unless you want to go your separate way," she adds.

"What?" Wes blurts out. "No." A growl escapes him. "Sorry." He clears his throat. "I mean, not yet, not until..."

But he doesn't finish, and I'm certain it's because he doesn't ever want to let her go.

A feeling I can only imagine is mutual between all of us.

"How do you plan on pulling this off, Birdie?"

"That parts easy. I've taken prisoners there before. This would be no different. These people trust my word, and if I have you in *my* captivity, they'll believe whatever it is I have to say."

That's right. She's their Furla Ain.

If anyone was going to pull this off, it would be her. But there's still the possibility that she's bluffing and scheming to walk us directly to our death. Why go through the trouble of faking these relationships with us though? Seems a bit too fucking elaborate if you ask me. But I guess that's my hopeful thinking at desperately wanting this all to be true. Her liking us, not her plotting our demise.

"And once we get to Rock Bridge?" Wes asks like he's actually considering her plan.

"I'm open to suggestions."

"Okay," is all he says.

"So, we're really doing this?" Dash takes a bite of his apple and leans back in his chair.

Wren's gaze meets mine, then Wes's. "I think so."

"Fuck it, I mean, what's the worst that could happen?" I reach across to snatch another chunk of the bread. If I'm going to my death, I'm sure as shit not doing it on an empty stomach.

16
WREN

I must have really lost my goddamn mind.

Not only have I invited three incredibly rare and powerful creatures into my home but now I am a willing participant in an elaborate scheme to rescue more of their kind. And I'm not just doing it for the cure. Sure, that's an added bonus, but after everything I've been through with them these past few days, I'm not so sure that someone who associates with them deserves to be in a place like Rock Bridge.

A prison-type fortress where demons go and never return.

The likelihood of their friends still being alive is slim to none, but I at least have to try. Especially when I am potentially capable of pulling this off.

The plan is simple enough. I fake that they are my prisoners and march them straight through enemy territory. I've done it before. So why wouldn't it work now? And if they question what took me so long or where I was in my absence, I have them as an alibi. Capturing all three of them would be no easy feat, giving my plan that much more validity. It's almost foolproof, really.

But I'd be lying if I said there wasn't an uneasy feeling rising in the pit of my stomach at putting their lives in danger like that.

I've run countless other scenarios through my head and none of them have the probability of success that this one does. The wendigo that has set its sights on us and the demon army following its command raise too many variables if we opt to take any other route than the direct one. Not knowing how many demons are on its side really throws a wrench in determining the risk factor. But at the end of the day, my title carries enough weight that the hunters that we no doubt will cross shouldn't question my authority. At least, that's what I'm fucking counting on.

I'm swallowing the last bite of my apple when a log bursts through the window in my kitchen, shattering the glass and landing with a thud onto the floor.

"What the fuck?" I hop to my feet as Wes and Bo mirror my movement, Dash following closely behind.

"Guess they have a witch after all." Bo slides the knife out of his waistband and grips the handle firmly. "Weapons?"

"This way." I wave for them to come with me,

ducking as another branch penetrates the same window, this one burning red hot with a flame.

Fucking assholes are going to burn my house down.

"They must not be able to get in, so they're trying to smoke us out," Wes announces on our way into my bedroom.

I rush over to the closet and press a panel on the back side. A compartment opens and I grip at the wooden slat to reveal my meager arsenal. It isn't much, but it's more than we were working with.

"Sick." Bo reaches for a compact crossbow. "I call dibs on this one."

"Grab whatever you can." I snatch a couple of my favorite blades first and secure them in place on my body. A person can never have enough knives. I slide out a sword and reach for the bag laying at my feet. The sound of chains clang from inside.

"What's that?" Wes asks me as he's stashing a blade into his waistband. His main weapon of choice is no doubt himself, considering he can set himself ablaze at a second's notice.

"Part of our ruse."

He tosses the strap over his shoulder and nods to the window I had escaped from when I overheard them whispering their secrets. "How far until we're in enemy territory?"

"Just on the other side of Wade Creek."

Another crashing commotion comes from the kitchen. They must be restricted to one area of the house if they haven't breached any other entry. The magical shield is partially in place, and if we're lucky, it'll hold long enough for us to get away.

Wes clutches my arm. "They're going to burn this place down. Is there anything you want to take with you?"

I stare up into his glowing eyes. "There's nothing here for me that can't be replaced."

Was this one of my favored safe houses? Yes, absolutely. But getting them out safely far exceeds any desire I have to keep this place standing.

"I'll go first." Bo reaches the window and grips at the base.

Wes stops him. "No, I can hold them off if they come."

"Will one of you fucking go?" I urge them.

Wes hops through and lands with a thud, glances around, and then reaches back in. "Come on." He drags Dash next, getting him safely outside my burning home. Smoke floats into my bedroom and flames nip at the doorway.

"You go first," I tell Bo, nudging him to the opening.

"Like hell, I will." Bo stands firmly in place.

"Go, you fucking stubborn idiot." I shove him. "Wes can heal me; he can't heal you." I guess it's one of the perks of being a fated mate of whatever Wes is. A mystery I've yet to uncover.

Hound, I recall him saying.

"One of you better hurry up before I come back in

there and drag you out myself." Wes frantically looks behind him and back at us. "*Move.*"

Bo grunts and shoves his large self through the small space, not fitting quite as easily as Wes had despite their similar size. Bo's shoulders must be a bit wider than Wes's. Although this is not the opportune time to realize such a thing.

Smoke continues to fill the room, more so now that Bo is blocking it from getting outside. The fire consumes the doorway, snaking itself up the wall, and dances across the ceiling in a kind of beautiful display.

"Uh, Bo, think you could suck it in and hurry up?"

"I'm trying, Birdie," he groans. His body slides slowly, inching further in the direction he needs to be going.

I shove at his large frame and hold my breath as my eyes begin to burn. They water and I close them in a weak attempt to protect them from the fumes.

Bo slips out the window and my body slams into the frame.

I blink through the tears and cough at the tainted air I sucked in from the impact.

A hand latches onto my forearm and when I squint, it's Wes pulling me through the window.

"Fuck, are you okay?" Wes holds onto my shoulders to steady me.

I nod and wipe at my eyes. "Yep, I'm golden." I point to the tree line ahead. "This way." I take off in that direction and glance behind me to make sure they're following.

Wes trails me closely with Dash in his wake, and Bo leading up the rear. Bo nods at me and I pick up the pace, grateful for the fresh air to fill my lungs despite the pain each labored breath causes me. Those fucking ribs are still broken from being crushed by that massive ogre. My poor body would be stoked to go a day without being injured in some insanely stupid capacity. How I'm still functioning is a shock to even me.

The night sky breaks with the promise of morning quickly approaching.

I was hoping we would have gotten the opportunity to rest in the safety of my home before embarking on the last leg of this journey, and maybe tie up a few loose ends on our half-assed plan, but that wendigo seized the chance to push us out while we were still weak. Clever thinking on its behalf, really. The demon is aware that we're powerful together, and it stands a much better chance of beating us in a weakened state. I was naïve for thinking we could rest when such a vile creature had begun its pursuit.

What can I say, I haven't exactly been at the top of my game lately with all the shit that's gone down.

I haven't recovered fully from the first incident, let alone the many that have followed.

And with Bo's venom still coursing through me, my hunter abilities aren't functioning the way they should.

A war cry rings out behind us as the demons realize

we've escaped through a blind spot in my magical concealment.

I push harder, but the spikes of pain make me lose steam quicker than I'd hope. I disassociate from it, shoving it into the furthest place in my mind, and kick my feet harder. Now is not the time to succumb to a little fucking discomfort. Not when we've already made it this far.

Something flutters in my peripheral and my instincts kick in all too late. The buzzing creature attacks, stinging me and moving on to another target. A swarm of the same kind follows and they all take turns assaulting whatever exposed flesh we have.

"We're almost there," I yell through the incessant high-pitched humming of the bee-like demonic creatures.

"What's stopping them from following us in?" Dash calls out from behind me.

"It's a one-way ticket," I pause to suck in a breath. "Only a hunter can get a demon out of sacred land. Can't you feel the barrier approaching?"

A loud roar rattles my ears, followed by the monstrous footsteps of a large creature.

I keep my eyes trained forward, not daring to turn around and look at what's pursuing us. Blisters and welts pop up all over my body and my face swells at being stung so many times. The stream, so close I can taste it, is our only chance of separating us from this torment.

The sound of flowing water soothes my soul, and the second I'm within range, I leap off the embankment and crash into the chilling liquid.

Another splash, followed by another. But the third doesn't come.

I frantically turn around, the current fighting me with every move. I scan the ridge, not waiting for the heads to appear from under the water to determine who didn't make it. My sights settle on a body almost completely covered in those hornets. I kick off the large rocks lining the stream and push toward the mound. Whoever it is, I refuse to leave them behind.

"Birdie, stop." Bo, water dripping over his long black locks, catches my hand and prevents me from going any further.

I try to yank free, but I can't. If he's here, that means it's either Dash or Wes out there in the danger zone. Just because Dash is a phoenix doesn't mean he should have to die because I can't save him. We know nothing about phoenixes. What if they only resurrect one time? Is that really a risk Bo is willing to take? Because it's not for me.

But my fears are erased when that mop of ginger hair gasps for air as he crashes through the surface of the water.

Another wave of terror flows through me when I realize Wes doesn't have that same skill that Dash does, and if he dies, it's possible he won't come back at all.

"Let go of me," I scream at Bo.

He shakes his head and latches onto me tighter. He nods toward the coast. "Just watch."

I look back to the sight of Wes being consumed by the buzzing beasts, my heart constricts at not being able to get to him. My lips part when the creatures start falling away, and in their place, a steaming orange light blasts through each crack until all of them drop to the ground and a blinding red emerges, flames completely dancing over Wes's exterior.

Slowly, he rises to his feet, setting fire to any leaves and grass he may touch. Flaming footprints remain with each step in his wake. He continues toward us and my mouth remains open in complete awe of how glorious his beastly side is.

Something I would have once found repulsive is now the most beautiful thing I've ever laid my eyes upon.

Wes drops into the water, his fire dwindling but still remaining like a protective shield. The closer he gets, the warmer the liquid becomes, until finally, he returns to his more human-looking self.

Bo releases me but I remain in place.

"Are you okay?" I mutter to Wes over the current rushing by.

He nods, his jaw clenched in a hard line.

I want to reach out to him, to pull him close and hold him tight and bask in his very existence, but there's no time for that when we're still dangerously near these demons. They might not be able to enter, but they can use their powers and weapons on us from this proximity.

Bo pulls Dash and the bag of chains up onto the bank on the other side of the stream. Marks litter both of them, but Bo's are vanishing from his own healing abilities.

I follow them out and shake my arms to rid myself of some of the excess water. I strain my hair and let out a breath. "There's a fountain up ahead, it will take care of this stuff." I motion to my face and look at Dash, who must be feeling like a hot bag of shit right now.

His eyes are nearly swollen shut, and his cheeks give off the impression that he's smuggling acorns in them.

"I can help you," Wes whispers.

But I shake my head, if Dash must suffer through this, then I will endure it with him.

We walk in silence to the spot I was referring to. The land grows quieter the further we go. The demons on our ass choosing not to pursue us in this demon-forsaken territory. At least one part of my plan has been a success, although getting here was a bit more stressful than I anticipated.

I cup the water from the fountain into my hand and splash it onto my face, showing them the magical effect it has. "See." I reach for Dash and rub some of the water onto his swollen arm and watch with him as the engorged skin goes back to how it once was.

"Wow," Dash whispers while dipping his arms completely into the fountain.

I savor the kid-like reaction and do the same, ridding myself of the painful blisters. It's not a moment later before we're both cleared of the stings.

"How did you know it would do that?" Dash stares at his forearm, turning it over and examining it from each direction.

I huff. "Not the first time I've been attacked by those stupid things." I recall one of the training sessions I had gone through when I was younger, where we encountered a smaller hive of those creatures and I was stung repeatedly on the face. I genuinely thought I was going to go blind until my instructor shoved my head into a fountain similar to this one on the far side of this territory. I sort of made it a point to track down the location of more of these just in case it happened again.

"Wes, Bo," Dash calls to the other guys. "You should try this."

Bo drops the bag of chains at my feet, ignoring Dash's amazement. "What's next, Birdie?"

I kneel and pry open the soaked top, reach in, and pull out a set of shackles. "These."

Bo takes them from me. "Kinky."

Leave it to him to say such a thing.

"Each of you, put a pair on." I give Wes and Dash theirs. "But don't clasp them." I tug out the long chain and secure it to their cuffs. "This is typically where I'd spell this to me, that way you can't get away, and it would diminish your power. But you aren't actually my prisoners, so we'll go ahead and skip that part."

"You're sure this is going to work?" Wes eyes me suspiciously.

No, not really, but I don't really see any other option available that doesn't immediately result in all our deaths.

"I've walked this path countless other times. I can't imagine this will be any different." It's not a lie, but I've never done it with three powerful beings that radiate so much demon energy that it's overwhelming. Any hunter in range will be alerted to the nearby threat and will no doubt want to come check it out for themselves.

I finish pretending to tie them up and toss the empty bag to the side. I sling the dagger over my shoulder and study the three of them. "I wouldn't make eye contact with any of the hunters if you can help it." I focus on Bo. "Do not draw attention to yourself."

Bo scrunches his bushy dark brows and points to his chest, his chain clanging from the motion. "Me?"

I tilt my head to the side and glare at him. "Yeah, you."

He rolls his eyes. "Whatever. I'll play along, don't worry."

Easier said than done when worry seems to be the one thing I'm excelling at.

"We need to get moving before someone comes looking for us. Once we've made it through the village, we'll have a moment to regroup before crossing into

Rock Bridge. Until then, keep your mouths shut, please." I don't mean for it to come out as harsh as it does, but if they rile up a hunter, there's no telling what kind of trouble they'll get us all in. The safest bet is for them to remain quiet and not cause any unnecessary drama. Their presence alone will drum up enough of it.

The walk into the town is filled with nervous energy.

The guys obey me by not speaking, but it doesn't manage to settle my anxiousness at all. I've never deceived my people before, especially with something so blasphemous as marching three unheard of demons through their encampment. I've taken prisoners to Rock Bridge in the past, but nothing like this.

The air radiates of hunter power and I can't help but wonder if they can pick up on the mark Bo left on my neck.

Heads turn when I step into view, but I carry on the same way I have every other time. I silently thank my past self for being so thorough in the manner I conduct business. Despite being recognized immediately, my peers are aware I prefer to deliver my targets prior to fraternizing and recharging at their various establishments. Even then, I typically keep to myself and stick to the bare necessities to get me by.

I carry the lead of the thick chain in my left hand and march through the middle of the road with my dagger over my right shoulder. I glance behind me and confirm that all three men are following closely, but not too close, behind. Their postures slack, their gaze averted to the ground. They look defeated, but that's all part of the act.

"Well, well, well, what do we have here?" A voice calls out.

I continue walking as a man I can't recall the name of jogs up to us.

"Quite the load you have there, Furla Ain. Need assistance?"

I glare at the on-comer and respond how I would any other time. "Does it look like I need help?"

He throws his pudgy hands up in the air. "Meant no offense, miss." He scans the men and his eyes narrow. He rubs at his chin. "Haven't seen one quite like this before." He approaches Wes a little too closely.

"I wouldn't do that if I were you," I warn him.

"Oh," he says with a bit of surprise. "You're telling me." He reaches toward Wes and clicks the lock on his shackle in place. "That could have been bad." He moves toward Bo next.

I stop and in one swift motion, point my dagger at his chest. "Don't patronize the way I do my job. I didn't get this title for nothing." I dig the tip of the blade into his armor, piercing it with ease. "Move along before I make you regret speaking to me."

The man blinks and steps back cautiously. "Very

well." He continues to backtrack until he turns around and scurries out of sight.

"Fucking bastard," I mutter under my breath. "We'll fix that later." I briefly glance at Wes's cuffs, which are now restricting his power.

He meets my gaze, and his glowing orbs tell me that he's not entirely powerless.

I grip the chains and tug the men behind me, hoping that another ignorant hunter doesn't try the same shit that one did. I catch glimpses of others as we pass by, but I don't pay any of them more than a lingering look.

A few minutes turn into what feels like a century of not knowing whether my acting is convincing enough. But why would these people assume anything other than the truth I'm giving them? How could I have become Furla Ain if I was anything other than a ruthless demon killer?

My hideous past is the one thing that's keeping this entire deception afloat.

It isn't until we're completely out of sight that I let out a breath and relax my shoulders. I go a little further into the thick forest between here and Rock Bridge, and guide the guys toward a set of trees.

"Wait here," I tell them. I point over to the path in the dirt. "I can get a better view from over there and see what we're working with." I shove my dagger toward Bo. "Hold this for me." I take off without another word, leaving them and the chains behind. Once I figure out how many guards are posted outside, we can come up with a plan of attack.

I rush over to the spot and cup my hand over my forehead to shield my eyes and get a better look. Three bodies pace the entrance of the fortress. It's possible we could eliminate them each and storm the place. But a subtle approach might be better. I could escort one of the guys in with me, tell the guards I'm delivering a prisoner, keeping true to the nature of my visit. Insisting that I have to bring the criminal directly to its holding cell, we could scout the other prisoners and find their people. I'd go in alone, but that would be a harder lie to sell.

A twig cracks behind me and when I turn, a familiar shape appears. Poker straight blonde hair, cut into an obnoxious bob, dressed head to toe in a dark blue pantsuit. Her serious expression slices through me like a knife.

"Parla," I mutter.

My fucking superior. One of them, at least. The eviler one of the two. Dravin looks the part, but he's a bit softer than Parla is. His bark is much feistier than his bite. Parla on the other hand, she's a fucking psychopath.

"Wren, darling." She smiles. "How lovely to see you. I was concerned when you hadn't checked in that you had fallen." She looks me up and down. "What a shame that would have been."

"Things were a bit more complicated than I antici-pated." My words are nothing but the truth.

"Hmm, I see." She shifts her focus to the watch on her wrist as it lights up briefly.

I use the distraction to subtly hold my hand down and signal to the guys to stay in place. If they're witnessing this, they're no doubt chomping at the bit to make a move.

"Where are they?" Parla cranes her neck to peer all around us.

With her back to me, I press my finger gently to my lips and stare in the direction of my men. "I already delivered them," I lie.

She narrows her pensive gaze at me. "You were ordered to kill on sight. You never disobey an order."

"My apologies, ma'am." My heart thumps wildly.

"Well then." Parla looks me up and down. "You must be punished for your insubordination."

If she knows what I think she does, then she's under the impression I just brought in one of the most powerful demons in our realm. And that still warrants punishment? But I can't exactly say that, because that would show my awareness of the situation, too.

Parla latches onto my wrist before I can process what's happening. "Wren Oliver, I hereby sentence you to a term at Rock Bridge, effective immediately."

"What? No. You can't be serious." I try to break free of her, but her grip is too tight.

"Do not talk back to me." Parla winds up her other

hand and smacks me across the face, knocking me to the ground.

I spit out blood and blink through the dusty dirt that flies up at me.

Shuffling of feet heightens my senses and when I look up, Wes is skidding to a halt in front of me. He mumbles a few words I can't decipher, and within seconds, I feel little layers of myself unlocking. My power comes back in full force, all the weakness I've had these last few days melts away until I'm almost completely returned to my hunter self.

Had he been suppressing my powers all along?

I shove the thought away because right now, none of that matters.

"Run, Wes, you have to run," I scream at him.

Parla laughs and mutters a spell. Sparks ignite from her fingertips and blast Wes in the chest, throwing him off balance.

"Stop it," I yell at her, jumping in the line of her attack. "Take me instead."

But whatever the magic is that she used renders both of us incapable of doing anything other than lay on the ground, writhing in agony, our arms outstretched toward each other, but not close enough to touch.

I stare into Wes's glowing eyes, the redness in them fading at not being able to access his other self.

"I'm sorry," he mouths to me.

She snaps her fingers together and a shadowy figure

appears beside her. "Find the rest of them," she orders the creature.

My heart rips in half. She's already gotten me, and she's taken down Wes. I burst through a layer of pain to scream as loudly as I can muster, "Guys, run!"

I'm met with a blow to the head, the painful sight of Wes becoming a blur and everything fading away.

To be continued in Fighting for Monsters, the second book in the Falling for the Enemy series...

Acknowledgments

What a fun one this was! This story and these characters have been simmering in my mind for a WHILE now and I am so stoked to finally bring them to life for you!

I hope I made you hate Bo, only to adore the shit out of his arrogant nature. Dash, the kind soul who I am so sorry for making you think was dead there for a minute. Wes, the poor guy is struggling so hard to figure out the right thing to do when his beast is clamoring for control. And Wren...she's a baddie but seriously has a long way to go with what's in store for her!

I have a long list of people I'd love to thank for being such rockstars, but I'll do my best to keep it short!

My kiddo.

My mom.

ViVi.

Tiffany.

Sarah. Deanna. Kate.

Sam. Michelle.

My incredible ARC & street teams!

Victoria. Clayton. James. Tyler.

All the folks from Tiktok who went wild when I told them about this story idea.

Night Witch for creating such a GORGEOUS cover!

And you, the reader—thank you for being here.

About the Author

Luna Pierce is a paranormal and contemporary romance author who loves getting lost in her stories. She brings you tough characters that love fiercely and fight for what's right, even if that means burning the city down for the ones they love. Luna adores all things gritty, and even supernatural.

When she's not writing, you'll find her consuming way too much coffee, making endless to-do lists, and spending time with her daughter and cats in small-town Ohio.

Join the exclusive reader group: Luna Pierce's Gritty Romance Squad

Join Luna's newsletter to receive updates at:
www.lunapierce.com/subscribe

Also by Luna Pierce

Falling for the Enemy

Fighting for Monsters (Book Two)

Fated to Monsters (Book Three)

The Harper Shadow Academy Series

(SET IN THE SAME STORY UNIVERSE AS STOLEN BY MONSTERS)

Hidden Magic (Book One)

Cursed Magic (Book Two)

Wicked Magic (Book Three)

Ancient Magic (Book Four)

Sacred Magic (Book Five)

Harper Shadow Academy: Complete Box Set

Sinners and Angels Universe

(DARK MAFIA CONTEMPORARY)

Broken Like You

Untamed Vixen

www.ingramcontent.com/pod-product-compliance
Lightning Source LLC
Chambersburg PA
CBHW030625190726
48286CB00008B/2397